THE

SIMON AND SCHUSTER

# To Mum

First published in Great Britain in 2013 by Simon & Schuster UK Ltd
A CBS COMPANY

1 3 5 7 9 10 8 6 4 2

Simon & Schuster UK Ltd
1st Floor
222 Gray's Inn Road
London
WC1X 8HB

www.simonandschuster.co.uk

Simon & Schuster Australia, Sydney

Simon & Schuster India, New Delhi

A CIP catalogue copy for this book is available from the British Library.

ISBN: 978-0-85707-864-3
eBook ISBN: 978-0-85707-865-0

Printed and bound in Great Britain by CPI Group (UK) Ltd, Croydon, CR0 4YY

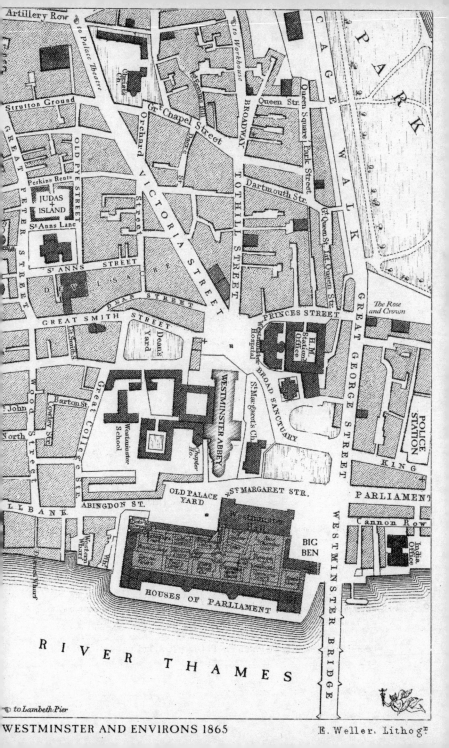

**WESTMINSTER AND ENVIRONS 1865**

E. Weller, Lithogr.

# 1

# SHELLS

The boy sat on the end of the jetty, skimming oyster shells across the water. It was too choppy to get many bounces but occasionally a shell would strike the dredger, moored further out, with a satisfying clang. He didn't even bother to prise open the next one before he threw it. The thought of slurping out its slick grey innards, still quivering, made him queasy. A person could get heartily sick of oysters, and Sammy often wished his father had been a cattle drover or a cheesemonger. Anything but an oyster farmer.

Now that he was eight he'd been given more responsibilities, including this afternoon's task of checking the size of the oysters seeded the previous week. He was taking as long as possible about it, to put off the moment he had to return to the shed to carry on de-barnacling with his brother. He'd been at it all morning and the icy water had made his hands too numb to feel when the knife slipped. It had taken this long for his fingers to warm up and now that the feeling had returned they were throbbing. He lowered them into the green water and threads of blood drifted out from them to coil around the oyster ropes. Like hair. Sammy shivered. He wished he hadn't thought of that: not now, not while he was out here all alone. The one who was killing all the children liked to take bits of their hair as a souvenir. That's why they called him the Wigman.

To try and drive the thought from his mind Sammy started whistling, a cheerful music-hall tune, but the sound drifted mournfully out over the dark water and he soon stopped.

The low sun burned crimson, glinting off the tips of the waves, and making the river appear to flow with blood. A few wisps of fog drifted in. If he waited a little longer he could say he'd got lost in it.

He realised he'd been too long when the water turned black. The fog had become so dense he couldn't see further than his own legs dangling over the jetty's edge, but if the sun had gone down it must be nearly five o'clock. His father would be furious. He'd probably have taken the cart and gone home, leaving Sammy to walk all the way back to Lambeth.

He scrambled to his feet and ran a little way along the slimy boards. Then skidded to a halt.

His father was waiting for him further down the jetty: he could just make out his blurred shape.

'I'm sorry,' Sammy called, 'I didn't know it was so late.'

He set off again, quicker. The fog enclosed him in a little bubble that contained only his scared breaths and the clatter of his footsteps along the boards.

'Tomorrow I'll start early and—'

He stopped. The shape had not moved, either to turn away in disgust or to raise a fist. It merely stood watching him, close now, but still veiled in smog. Perhaps it was a policeman.

'Excuse me, sir,' he said as he hurried up alongside the figure, 'but my father is waiting for me.'

The figure moved sharply and Sammy went sprawling.

'Hey!' he cried as he was roughly turned over, but the cry was cut short as rags were thrust into his mouth and a cord tied around his head to keep them in place.

Then the man was gone. Sammy lay there a moment in bewilderment, then sat up. The rags were packed so tightly he could hardly breathe. They tasted of honey.

Too late he heard the crunch of pebbles below. The man had merely jumped off the pier onto the beach. Hands reached up and yanked him over. Throwing out his arms to save himself he landed heavily on his wrist, and it gave an audible crack. His scream was muffled by the rags.

As pain overwhelmed him, he was dimly aware of being dragged up the beach and laid down. Then something heavy and smelling of sweat was thrown over him and he was left in darkness.

He knew immediately what was happening. The Wigman had got him. Over the thumping of his heart he could hear the man chanting, a little way off.

Biting his lip to suppress the cries of pain and terror, Sammy used his good hand to lift the coat off. Everything was grey. The smog would shield him from sight and muffle the sounds of his escape. He rolled onto his stomach, then pushed himself up onto all fours. The wall swung into view beside him, wet and black with algae. There were some steps fifty or so yards east of the pier. He began to crawl towards them.

The sand beneath his knees was stinking and black, with tar and muck from the tanner's yard and slaughterhouse.

There was a splash some way behind him and the voice intoned, '*Accept this gift.*' Sammy moved quicker, his left wrist flapping uselessly. A moment later another splash, more distant now. '*Accept this gift.*' Closer and clearer were the booms of Big Ben striking a quarter past the hour. Would his father have gone home or was he on his way here now, his fists rolled and ready? Sammy hoped it was the latter, and was momentarily glad that the Wigman had taken him: at least it was an acceptable excuse.

The wall suddenly zigzagged up away from him. He had reached the steps.

Climbing onto the first tread he allowed himself a moment's relief. Very few had escaped the Wigman to tell the tale, and most of those had wriggled out of his arms before he could do any tying up and chanting. But here Sammy was, nearly free, and with a story that would bathe him in adulation for years to come.

Then he heard voices from above, the first deep and gravelly:

'Can't see him. Fog's too deep.'

The second a bad-tempered whine:

'Prob'ly home by the fire, eating bread and dripping.'

It was his father and brother. He tried to call out to them but his muffled squeak from beneath the gag was drowned by the tidewash.

'He might have fallen asleep on the pier. We shouldn't leave him.' His father again.

'He deserves it. He never does his fair share. I have to work twice as hard to make up for him.'

'He ain't as old as you.'

'Ain't far off. You're too soft on him.'

Sammy wasted a few seconds fumbling at the knot round the back of his head, then continued to climb. It was hard, with only one good hand and the steps so slippery.

'Come on, Pa,' his brother said. 'Let's get on. If he is asleep it'll teach him a lesson.'

'I'm not sure. Not with this Wigman feller about.'

Sucking in as much air as he could through soot-coated nostrils Sammy shouted, 'Dad! Fred!'

It came out as 'Ahhhg! Ehhhh!' but would have been audible, had a barge not come by at just that moment and given several long honks on its horn.

'Asleep?' Fred sniggered. 'On a night like this, with the boats sounding their warnings every five minutes? I tell you, he's home with Ma. Let's go.'

Sammy hauled himself up the next few steps. He was more than halfway now, but could hear his father's heavy footsteps retreating.

He shouted for him to wait.

'Aiighhh!'

The footsteps were growing fainter, but it was all right. He could still catch up with them and bring his father back to the beach. The Wigman wouldn't know what had hit him.

A blow sent Sammy reeling sideways and he crashed down onto the sand, too winded even to scream.

He looked up mutely at his assailant. The Wigman was younger than they said, not more than twenty or so. His face was utterly colourless, like a grub dug up from the soil, and glistened like sweaty lard as the man knelt down beside him. His hands were massive, red and scarred, and Sammy watched in horror as he slipped one of them into his pocket and drew out a knife. He brought it towards Sammy's face. Sammy screwed up his eyes and moaned, but with a flick of the wrist all the man took was a hank of hair.

As the Wigman was tucking the lock into his pocket, Sammy brought his knee up sharply and the knife skittered across the sand. Sammy flipped himself over and went after it, grunting as his wrist collapsed and he lurched sideways, but righting himself and clawing onwards.

The knife glimmered on the black sand and Sammy's fingers were almost touching it when he was hauled into the air. With his good arm he clawed at the Wigman's eyes and throat but the arm was clamped down and his face was pressed into a chest that stank of tallow and sweat. Sammy sank his teeth into the soft flesh until a fist descended on his head.

The blow and the lack of air were making him dizzy and he began to see strange things in the darkness: shadowy figures gathered at the edges of his vision, murmuring to one another. Or was that just the shush of the river on the beach?

The murmuring grew louder and the cold air slapped him alert as he landed on the sand. Water lapped around him, filling his ears, seeping into his clothes. The Wigman knelt down next to him, cut the cord around his head and pulled the rags from his mouth.

'Let me go, please,' Sammy gasped. 'My father's rich, he'll pay you whatever you ask, I won't say who you are I swear . . .'

But the man wasn't listening. He reached into his pocket again, took out an object and pushed it into Sammy's open mouth. The slick congealed thing slipped straight to the back of his throat, its end fitting snugly into the opening of the airway. Then the hands launched him out into the dark water.

Escape was still possible. He could swim well. He would simply roll onto his stomach, cough out the thing, whatever it was, and make for the other shore.

Then something heavy fell across his abdomen and he went under.

As the water surged into his nostrils he looked up to see the shadow of the Wigman step back, leaving just the fog, now endless green stretching all the way to the sky.

# 2

# THE PALACE THEATRE

'Mother!' Titus said for the third time.

One of the shrouded shapes on the bed finally stirred.

He tugged the stained sheet down to reveal his mother's face: the evening sunlight falling on her cheek gave it a deceptively healthy glow.

'Have you seen Hannah?'

Next to her the other shape rolled over and a sour smell, of sweat and drink and urine, wafted from the blanket. There was no sense trying to ask his father anything so he shook his mother's bony shoulder until she peeled one eyelid up.

'Has she been back here?'

'Ungh.'

He went to the window and pulled back the rag, tucking it behind the songbird's cage. As usual three wan children sat in the window of the house opposite, staring at the little yellow bird. The houses leaned into one other so much that occasionally Titus would unhook the cage and hold it out for them to poke their fingers inside, thinking it might make them smile. It never did.

But there wasn't time for playing now. Titus had returned from delivering some mended shirts to find his sister missing. She was supposed to have spent the day sewing. Until Titus found himself some proper employment, mending other people's clothing was the only source of income in this household – though it was left to him and Hannah to do it, as these days his parents were dead drunk by noon and asleep by four. Normally his sister's disappearances just infuriated him, but it was six thirty now and he hadn't seen her since lunchtime and, what with all the murders, he was starting to get worried.

'Mother!' He went back to the bed. 'Wake up and do some work!'

This time she didn't even stir.

He swore to himself, threw the sheet back over her head and made for the stairs.

As soon as he stepped out into the alley the wind rushed at him, finding all the holes in his clothes and worming into them. It was strong enough to have blown the smog away and directly above him the little patch of sky visible between the roofs was a beautiful clear violet.

He didn't have time to admire it. He set off down the alley in the direction of the river.

This time when he found Hannah he'd give her a proper hiding. Like Father used to with his belt. Titus had tried reasoning with her and extracting promises but neither had had any effect other than to make him look like a sap. Stitcher, in comparison, probably seemed like the height of rakish glamour to her, with his silk cravat and mother-of-pearl pocket watch making him look far more sophisticated than his fifteen years.

At the end of Old Pye Street, Titus took a left into Perkins Rents and headed for the ramshackle mansion where Stitcher lived with his 'family': a menacing crew of pickpockets, tarts, professional beggars and other boys who lived off their wits. The area beneath the house was honeycombed with tunnels to elude police.

The door stood half open but there was little light coming from inside. The inhabitants tended to sleep during the day. Titus stepped into the gloomy interior. A line of stolen white silk handkerchiefs ran the length of the hall, like ghostly bunting. The windows had recently been patched with newspaper and the face of the Wigman leered out at him, swarthy and low-browed; more like a monkey than a man. Of course the woodcut was all guess-work. No-one really knew what he looked like, and there were plenty who didn't even think he was human. The artist was clearly very skilled, however: the black eyes were cold and cruel and horribly alive.

A creak of floorboards above his head made him jump.

'Hannah?' he called up the stairs.

A minute later, a white face swam up out of the gloom of the first-floor landing.

'Oh, hello, Titus,' a woman's voice croaked.

It was Rosie, bleary-eyed. She must have been sleeping off her last client.

'You lost Hannah again?'

He blushed at the sight of her in her petticoat and looked at the floor. At seventeen she was only two years older than him but she looked like a full-grown woman.

'Any idea where they've got to, Rosie?'

'I think Stitcher mentioned some show on at the Palace. They're expecting a big crowd.'

'The Palace? On Victoria Street?'

# A CHANCE TO SEE WITH YOUR OWN EYES THE
# PHENOMENON
## THAT IS
# SIGNORINA VASO

## NO TRICKS! NO PROPS!
### GENUINE COMMUNING WITH SPIRITS.
### FROM ANCIENT ROMANS TO
### OUR BRAVE HEROES OF THE CRIMEA

# BE ASTOUNDED!
## PERHAPS SHE WILL HAVE A MESSAGE FOR YOU!

# PALACE THEATRE, VICTORIA STREET
## Friday 20th October at 7-30 Admission 4d.

She nodded and stretched, then trailed back to her bedroom.

'Thanks!' he called after her, then raced out into the street.

As he came out onto Victoria Street the dirty and tumbledown piles that crowded the narrow alleys gave way to modern white-stucco mansions, theatres and glittering public houses. The gas lamps had been lit, and well-dressed people ambled towards Westminster Bridge, the tips of their canes and gold watches aglow.

Even now, so long after having forsworn the bad ways of his past, Titus couldn't help noticing the handkerchiefs hanging out of pockets and the silk umbrellas held so loosely.

A bill pasted to a wall on the other side of the street caught his eye and he dodged the traffic to get across to it. He'd only had six months in the Ragged School and the words were such a jumble of colours and sizes that it took him some minutes to work out what it said: The medium, Signorina Vaso, was apearing at the Palace tonight – at 7.30 pm.

He squinted up at the face of Big Ben – twenty past seven – and started running.

There was still a queue outside when he reached the theatre, and they all looked mighty respectable. Nobody was pushing or queue-jumping or shouting at the people in front to hurry up. Stitcher's mob would stick out amongst this lot like a bunch of sore thumbs.

An elderly woman in a tasselled shawl was saying to the woman next to her, 'Of course Doctor Magnusson tells me these shows are simply the worst for my nerves, but you just can't keep away, can you? And this girl's supposed to be extraordinary . . .'

The queue moved forward sedately and, peering over the hats and bonnets, Titus could see that the theatre foyer was in almost total darkness. Rich pickings if the gang had managed to sneak in another entrance.

He went down the alley on the left of the building but the only windows were high in the wall and too small even for Stitcher's little brother and main accomplice, Charly. Doubling back, Titus tried the alley on the other side. He was in luck. Down at the far end light spilled from an open doorway.

Only as he was about to slip inside did Titus notice the thread of tobacco smoke rising into the air from the shadows.

'Don't even think about it.'

A man stepped forward, dressed in a tailcoat and top hat.

'You want to come in, you pay like the rest.'

He was trying to cover his accent but Titus could hear it smearing the edges of his clipped words, and now that he looked more closely he could see something of the slums in the man's gimlet eyes and hard mouth. His face was pasty and pocked but it had merged into the shadows, thanks to the coarse black hair that covered his cheeks and chin and came down low on his forehead. In contrast the man's lips were a moist blood-red. He licked them before spitting onto the ground.

If he'd been a real gentleman Titus might have stood a chance of talking his way in, but he was pretty sure this one had the measure of him already so, with a curl of his lip, Titus turned and headed back the way he had come.

The queue was gone now and the foyer was filled with shifting shadows. The occasional brooch or brass handle gleamed in the low lantern light but the room might as well have been filled with a mass of crawling beetles. As Titus crossed the threshold, a sharp-faced usher gripped his arm.

'Ticket.'

Titus stood up straight and gave the boy an aggrieved look.

'I ain't here for the show. I been sent to find Doctor Magnusson. The Duke's taken a turn for the worse.'

The usher's eyes widened.

'You seen him?' Titus went on urgently. 'Tall feller, top hat, beard. Looks grand, like.'

The usher frowned. 'I think so . . . Did he have a big black bag with him?'

'That's him! Thank the Lord.'

Titus patted the boy on the shoulder and pushed his way into the foyer. The atmosphere in there was charged with excitement. For the next ten minutes he milled around, following the ebb and flow of the crowd impatient to enter the auditorium. This was where they'd be, in amongst it all, where gentlemen touching hip-to-hip wouldn't feel their pocket watches gently slipping away, and ladies wouldn't notice the sudden lightness of their arm where a moment ago a purse had dangled. But he didn't run into them and, more tellingly, there were no cries of fury or surprise. Once he dropped to his knees and peered through the legs – Charly barely came up to an adult's hip – but there was no sign of them. The only other possibility was that they might be holed up under the seats in the auditorium itself. A few minutes later the auditorium doors opened and Titus allowed himself to be carried with the surge.

Those in front of him rushed forward and those behind thrust at his back until he was inexorably carried to the front rows. Only as he was driven down the third row from the front and came face to face with those galloping up from the opposite aisle did he realise he was trapped. Somebody thrust him down into a seat in order to scramble over him to the one on the other side and soon he was surrounded.

Turning round he saw a thousand wide eyes, glittering in the gloom, all staring at the stage.

He turned back. Having worked a few medium shows before he was a little surprised by what he saw. The chair positioned on the dais was a simple wooden thing, more at home in servants' quarters than here. And that was the only item of furniture he could make out. Where was the cabinet? These, he had thought, were *de rigueur* for every medium worth the name. At some point in the séance the medium would conceal herself inside and then various spirits would emerge to speak their divine truths. Coincidentally these spirits usually bore no small resemblance to the medium herself, with a few more veils and perhaps an Egyptian-style wig. But the cabinet was not there. Neither was there a table with a conveniently draping cloth, a shadowy assistant, nor any of the accoutrements usually employed to hoodwink an audience: just the chair and the plain back wall of the stage. There was a little more light than was usual too: a lantern on either side of the room and a line of candles on the edge of the stage. Even the curtains had been tied back as if to show that no-one was hiding amongst their folds.

The loud bang made him jump and a rustle passed through the audience as all heads turned at once.

The man who had been smoking at the stage door was now standing at the back of the auditorium.

'Ladies and gentlemen. Welcome to the Palace Theatre. As you can see,' he held up a bunch of keys which glimmered in the lantern light, 'I have just locked you all in.'

A murmur shivered around the audience.

'The stage manager has kindly permitted me to take charge of the only set of keys, which will hang on my waistcoat until the very end of the séance. No man, woman or child will be allowed in or out of this room, except under the direst of circumstances, and thus you may have total confidence that no-one can steal in to assist Signorina Vaso. Now then,' he lowered his voice, 'I know you have all heard of Summerland. That paradise where spirits bask in eternal peace, free from care and sorrow . . .'

A few nods from the audience.

'Well, the spirits you will meet tonight have not yet passed on into that blessed realm. They are lost souls. Suffering and afraid. I must warn you that the spectacle you are about to witness may be disturbing, even terrifying.'

He paused to allow his words to take their full dramatic effect.

Titus settled back into his seat. It looked as if he was here for the duration.

'Anyone having second thoughts, all those who possess a fragile disposition, any lady who might be with child, I ask that you please leave now.'

Nobody moved.

'Very well. We will begin.'

With that he crossed his arms behind his back and gave his full attention to the stage.

As everyone followed his lead, cries of surprise went up from some of the ladies. The chair on the stage was now occupied, by what appeared at first glance to be a ghost.

Titus smiled. A clever little trick to get them all in the mood. Perhaps it wouldn't be a wholly wasted hour after all; perhaps he might actually enjoy himself.

The girl was thin and pale as a pipe stem. She had nothing on but a white nightdress that only came down to her knees. Mediums liked to do that sort of thing to prove they weren't hiding any props. Her head was bent and she gripped her knees so tightly Titus could see the tendons springing out on the backs of her hands. When she eventually looked up Titus saw that she was no older than he, delicately pretty but with large shadows bruising her cheeks and eye sockets.

Her eyes were huge as they stared into the darkness. The candles at the front of the stage made her own shadow on the back wall seem to loom over her. A soft breeze disturbed her fine black hair and Titus glanced round to see if the doors had been surreptitiously opened. They had not.

When he turned back she had closed those disconcerting eyes and placed her hands palm up in her lap.

'Florence, are you there?'

Her voice was much stronger than her frame would suggest. It bounced off the walls and high ceiling and in the silence that followed its echoes seemed to go on forever. The concentrated hush of the room pressed so hard on Titus's temples he felt dizzy. Then she took a great gasping breath and opened her eyes.

'I am here.'

Though her lips moved in perfect synchronicity with the words, it was impossible to believe she had spoken them. This new voice was extremely old and had a Scottish lilt. Presumably this was the 'Spirit Guide', who would mediate between herself and the Other Side. Titus was half-impressed that she hadn't picked the usual 'Arab Prince' or 'Egyptian Queen'. He glanced behind him again to try and see which plant in the audience was throwing her voice. Without exception all faces were rapt, all mouths hung open.

'Is anyone with you?' This was the medium herself again. Titus leaned forward and squinted into the darkness. Was someone crouched on the floor? Or was there some kind of grille allowing an accomplice to speak from an anteroom?

'Edwin,' the old woman said. 'He has a message for his mama.'

Titus jumped as a woman behind him gave a stifled yelp.

'Edwin wishes you to know that he did not suffer, since the musket bullet penetrated his brain in such a way that death was instantaneous. He wants your assurance that you will endeavour to live happily again before he can pass over.'

For a moment the room was silent and then a choked voice said:

'He has it.'

A sigh passed over the company. Before Titus could catch his breath the spirit guide spoke again.

'Clara is here.'

18

No sound came from the audience.

'Clara wishes to tell her sisters that she is at peace now and hopes they can forgive her.'

Poor Clara's loved ones were clearly absent because when her name elicited no howls or shrieks a ripple of impatience passed through the crowd.

As the show went on, various names were hazarded with varying degrees of success. Even when no-one owned up to a particular spirit, Signorina Vaso would continue with the message, as if that were the important part of the night's proceedings rather than the entertainment of the crowd.

Titus grew bored. He picked at a threadbare patch of velvet on the arm of his seat.

'Is there a Titus in the room?'

His heart tried its very hardest not to stop dead.

'An old friend has a message.'

He attempted a sneering grin but his lips peeled back from his teeth.

'Ronnie says to keep your wits about you because there's something big coming your way.'

He almost laughed out loud in relief. The only Ronnie he knew was Ronnie Black: alive and well and living in Bristol. He'd left Stitcher's gang not long before Titus and gone off to try his luck in the shipyards. He'd tried to persuade Titus to go too, but the shipyards were no place for a girl of nine and he wasn't going to leave Hannah behind.

The medium moved on but Titus couldn't shake the feeling of unease. He tried to tell himself she'd just plucked a likely name from the air (no doubt everyone in the room knew a Ronnie) but she'd certainly seemed to be directing her speech to him. And the way she'd seemed to still be looking at him, even though her eyes were closed, brought goosebumps up on his arms

Murmurs from the crowd snapped his attention back to the dais. Something was happening to the Signorina's face. The prettiness had entirely gone from her and her flesh had congealed into something resembling a death mask. Her eyes were glazed, her body rigid against the chair back. From somewhere deep down in her throat there came a grunting, choking sound.

Abruptly her head was wrenched back and the audience gasped. Something large and writhing was making its way up her throat. Titus could not take a breath as the thing made its way into the medium's mouth, pushing her swollen tongue out like a strangulation victim. And then white froth appeared at her lips. No, no, it was more fluid than that; like cream. Although cream would not slither down her chin and then rear up to sway a pointed tongue at the audience as if tasting them.

It was ectoplasm. Though he'd heard of it he'd never seen anyone try to do it before. It must be white ribbon, swallowed in a ball and then slowly unravelled . . . But wait, now something else was happening. It couldn't be ribbon for now the white material spread out and seemed to drape itself over a human body.

It was a child, but not an infant: nine or ten Titus guessed. Too large to conceal without someone noticing. He shuffled down in his seat as the figure went suddenly still, as if seeing for the first time the crowd of people observing it.

'Dad?'

It was the tremulous voice of a frightened child.

The approximation of a face scoured the room, pausing interminably on each terrified countenance.

'He's got me, Dad!' the child's voice cried. 'Come quick or he'll do me like the rest!'

A woman behind him gasped. 'He means the Wigman!' she hissed to her friend. 'Perhaps he'll reveal his identity!'

But now the shape was backing away, raising hands to its face as if to ward off a blow. The figure merged with the edge of the stage and Titus watched transfixed as the flame of the candle burned for a moment inside its chest before guttering and going out.

This display of anguish was too much for a woman in the front row.

'You poor wretch!' she wailed and flung herself at the stage, arms extended. But the apparition had vanished. The woman's arms wheeled through darkness and she crashed to the floor. The lamps were turned up and men rushed to her aid. A moment later she and the now-senseless Signorina were carried from the room, and the subdued audience filed out after them.

Emerging from the auditorium into the relative brightness of the foyer was like bursting out of stagnant water into fresh air.

Titus needed a drink. Back when his mother only took it to help her sleep he'd enjoyed a glass or two of gin with her before bed, but after seeing what it did to her he'd forsworn it. He passed through the few remaining audience members towards the doors. The mood was subdued. Most stood around staring into the glasses of wine brought round on a tray by the usher. Titus ducked behind a pillar, but the boy was pale and kept forgetting to ask his customers for payment, so didn't spot him. A few people whispered breathlessly to one another. Those women the medium had addressed directly were crying.

On a high table near the doors two glasses of wine sat, forgotten, while their owners compared how much one another's hands were shaking. Titus picked up one of the glasses and tossed it back. Then he went back for the second.

Out on the street he leaned against a wall and closed his eyes. Dizziness from the wine added to the shock of the séance was making him nauseous. He wanted to go home to bed. But if he got home and Hannah wasn't there he'd just have to go out looking for her again.

He sighed and opened his eyes. The street lights were bright against the black sky and the few well-to-do people still out were hailing cabs. It must be getting late. Stitcher and his gang didn't go out at night – they left that sort of work, the sort that would get you hanged, to the older, harder men. If Hannah had been out pickpocketing with them there was only one place she was likely to be by now.

He pushed himself off the wall and started walking in the direction of King Street police station.

# 3

# INSPECTOR PILBURY

'Is she here?'

The copper on the front desk nodded: 'Out back with the Inspector. I believe they're discussing the various merits of plums versus greengages.'

'Has he charged her?'

The copper chuckled. 'What do you think?'

He unlocked the door to the right of the desk and Titus thanked him and walked through.

Long before he saw his sister he could hear her, mouthing off in that insistent high-pitched gabble about how if she had a police station she'd make the officers wear red so they would look bold and dashing like soldiers. He clenched his teeth and stalked down the corridor to the kitchen.

Hannah sat swinging her legs on the kitchen table, giving Inspector Pilbury the benefit of her wisdom between mouthfuls of plum. A bowl sat next to her, filled with nothing but plum stones. She had eaten all the officers' fruit. A flush of fury and embarrassment rushed up Titus's neck.

The Inspector, smoking by the fire in his shirtsleeves, saw Titus first.

'Look lively, Hannah,' he said. 'The guvnor's here.'

Hannah jumped off the table as if it had been suddenly turned to hot iron.

'I didn't do nothing,' she said. 'I was just there, like, that's all.'

'Evening, Inspector,' Titus said, standing a little straighter. 'Thanks very much for looking after her.'

'Oh, she's been looking after me. If it wasn't for your sister I'd never have known cholera could be caught from pigeons.'

'Please excuse her ignorance, sir, she'd rather be hanging about with thieves and no-hopers than going to school.'

Hannah opened her mouth to speak but changed her mind.

'Ah well,' the Inspector sighed, knocking his pipe out against the fireplace, 'I suppose this charming interlude must come to an end.'

He got up and wandered over to the window that looked out on the prison yard and cells.

'Come on!' Titus hissed at Hannah. 'And I hope you thanked him for all them plums.'

'I was bloody starving,' she squealed. 'I ain't eaten nothing since yesterday morning.'

He took her by the arm, a little too roughly for she winced in pain and then her lip began to wobble.

'Oh don't start,' he muttered and led her towards the door at the back of the room: they could go out through the yard gate.

The Inspector was deep in thought, his face expressionless as he stared out. He was tall and thin but this slenderness did not mean weakness. The muscles of his biceps strained at the fabric of his shirt, the veins snaking up them like ropes. His hands were large and red and might easily have belonged to a hardened villain, but their colour did not extend to the rest of him. His face was grey and his jaw shadowed, as if his teeth were permanently clenched.

'Thanks again, sir. And thanks for not charging her. Next time I reckon you ought to. It might change her bad ways.'

'She's not bad, Titus. I should know.'

He turned and gave the children a wan smile. It was that sad, kindly face that had so entranced Hannah the first time she saw him.

During one of their parents' bitterest disputes the police had been called and the whole family were transported to the station. While the adults had been confined to the cells, Titus and Hannah were settled in front of the kitchen fire with teacakes and mugs of cocoa. God knows what it was that entranced Inspector Pilbury about his cocky little sister, but he'd had a soft spot for her ever since that first meeting. Tonight she'd probably hung around after the rest of the gang had scarpered and got herself caught deliberately, just so she could get a meal in the warm.

Frankly he didn't mind too much. In fact he was so glad to be spending a moment or two with the Inspector, he was finding it hard to stay angry with her.

'We'll be off then, and I swear you won't be seeing Hannah again.'

Glancing briefly at his hand and deciding it was adequately clean, he held it out to the older man.

'Oh I do hope that's not the case,' Pilbury said, taking it, then frowning.

'Good God, boy, you're freezing. Sit a moment by the fire and warm up before you go.'

'No, no. I'm fine, really, sir . . .' he began weakly but did not protest as Hannah dragged him over to the chair the Inspector had just vacated, then settled herself on the floor and began drawing in the ash that spilled across the flagstones.

'Perhaps just a few minutes . . .'

The chair was soft and smelled deliciously of pipe smoke. The Inspector's coat hung on the back; a pair of handcuffs protruding from the left-hand pocket glittered in the firelight. The flames were mesmerising, crackling lullabies. At home the cot was far too small for the both of them and Titus often slept on the floor, which was hard and draughty and crawling with cockroaches.

He blinked and shook the drowsiness out of his head. If the hiding he was going to give Hannah when they got home had the desired effect this might be the last time he'd have to fetch her from the station, and his last chance to speak to Mr Pilbury.

But before he could open his mouth there came the rumble of men's voices outside the door. A moment later it burst open and the policemen poured in, like a great blue wave breaking on the room. They tramped over to the table, one of them carrying a tray of meat puddings, and settled down amidst much thumping and squealing of chairs.

'Line your stomachs, lads,' the Inspector said. 'God knows what you might find over there.'

One of the younger ones looked up. 'Do you think there might be more bodies then, or the hair?'

'Who knows,' Pilbury said. 'But if the mother's as bad

as they say you might find a few things that'll turn your stomach.'

'My stomach's clad with iron,' another man cried. 'So chuck us one of those, Samson, before it cracks in half!'

The officer called Samson ignored him and turned to the Inspector. 'What would you like, sir? There's steak and onion, lamb and mint or pork and apple.'

'Not for me. I'm up to my chin in pies and tarts.'

'Mrs Membery?'

Pilbury smiled. 'God bless her.'

'Well, don't tell her, but I think the steak and onion beats even her best efforts. Won't you give it a try?'

Samson's words were light but Titus thought the glance he gave his superior showed a flicker of anxiety.

'I'll have something when you men have gone.'

The pies were distributed and the men tore into them. Hannah resumed drawing in the cinders, but Titus could not take his eyes off the policemen. The way they sat, chatting and laughing, eating and wiping their mouths like any other human creature, seemed at odds with the sheer wonderfulness of their appearance. Their uniforms were velvet blue, their buttons flashed, their boots shone. But though they were all equally fine in appearance Titus had come to understand there was a strict hierarchy of authority. Some of them had gold chevrons on their sleeve. Samson had two, making him a sergeant. The Inspector had three, which meant he was the most important, though you would never know it from his humble manner; only these markings and the men's deference.

'Do you reckon there's more, sir, then, than what's been discovered?' one of them said between mouthfuls.

Pilbury shrugged.

'Let's hope not, but no-one ever reports these street children missing.'

'There was that one father as did. The oyster catcher from Lambeth.'

'They found that one,' another chipped in. 'Don't you remember? Under the boat beam by the pier. His nose nibbled off by the eels.'

The men jumped as the Inspector gave a hiss and glanced at Hannah, but she was too busy with her drawings to pay any attention.

The door to the yard opened and a boy not much older than Titus came in. His hair was as orange as scallop roe and his face a mass of large freckles. One of his left incisors stuck out from the others, lifting his lip in a sneer.

'Ooh, lovely. Any steak and onion?' he said, thrusting himself between the men.

'There's pork and apple or nothing,' Samson said. 'And you should be thankful for it. A policeman's wages isn't enough to cover the feeding of greedy stable boys.'

'I think you'll find I am a groom,' the boy replied. 'Like what the Queen has.'

Samson curled his lip but let the comment pass. The boy took the pie, smeared it with mustard and went to sit on the window seat, his dirty boots resting on the white sill.

'Right,' Sergeant Samson barked. 'Let's get this over with.'

The men rose from the table.

'Fetch your helmets and lanterns,' said Samson. 'And I want everyone to bring their batons. We don't know how strong he'll be.'

As the men were filing out the Inspector added quietly:

'Your pistols too.'

There were astonished murmurs from the men.

'Yes, sir,' Samson said and the men departed, with Pilbury following. As he passed the children he slipped something into Titus's hand. A penny. Titus thrust it into his pocket before the stable boy could see.

For a while there was just the crackling of the fire, but then the stable boy broke the silence.

'He's mad.'

Titus turned to see him regarding them from the windowsill.

'The Inspector. Letting you two thieving scroungers come beggin' here all the time.'

Hannah's sooty finger stopped dead in the act of drawing the pupil of a pony's eye. Titus stared at him, all drowsiness swept away in a surge of anger.

'We're not thieves,' he said quietly. 'Or beggars.'

'My arse!' the boy snorted.

He ran his tongue down his protruding tooth. Titus looked at him for a moment, then turned back to the fire. Hannah jerked her chin towards the door that led back through the station but Titus shook his head. If they slunk away now it would be as good as admitting they were cowards as well as thieves.

For a moment there was silence but for the stable boy slurping up the pie. Eventually the slurping stopped and the boy slapped his hands together. Titus heard his footsteps approaching and the boy swaggered into his line of vision.

'I heard your old man's mad as a hatter. Is it true he once jumped into the Thames to escape marauding Russians?'

This was not true. Their father had turned to face his imaginary foe with a poker and a carving knife and was forcibly disarmed by the police. It had taken three of them. Back then his father was hale and strong; he had returned from the Crimea unharmed in body, but what he had seen had so injured his mind that only the oblivion brought on by drink could ease his suffering. Titus could not blame him for it, nor even his mother who had dealt with her husband's spiralling insanity the same way. It angered Titus that the sacrifices of people like his father had been forgotten: instead of being lauded as heroes they had become objects of distrust and ridicule.

He stood up, and Hannah rose to stand beside him.

'You great fat—' she began but Titus hushed her.

'He's a good father and was a brave soldier,' he said, holding the boy's gaze. As there was almost a foot between them this meant he had to look down a little, but this would be no advantage in a fight: the boy must weigh several stones more.

'Brave like you, you mean? Hiding behind your sister?'

Titus sighed. 'Come on, Hannah.'

'That's right, run away, like your dad!'

As they stepped out into the courtyard a blow to his back sent Titus stumbling forwards. Pushing Hannah aside he turned round. The stable boy swaggered towards him, his fists drawn up to his chest.

Titus sized him up. He was too bulky to be fast, plus he was now heavy with the pie. Titus would be quicker, but lack of food meant his stamina would drain quickly.

He didn't actually want to hurt him. In fact he was grateful the boy had chosen this way to try and humiliate him. A far more effective method would have been simply to make his comments in front of the Inspector.

He backed away and positioned himself in a patch of shadow. The boy's face in the light from the kitchen was a round moon, his eyes wide as he tried to pick out the contours of Titus's frame. Finally he came at him, his fat fist pulled back behind his shoulder.

The blow to his solar plexus sent the boy reeling back. He struck the stable wall and crumpled, gasping for air with little squealing noises, like a newborn piglet.

Hannah was laughing from the threshold of the kitchen but Titus hushed her. The insult was paid for. There was no need to crow about it.

When the boy was able to breathe again Titus helped him up, then turned and headed back to Hannah. But as he walked towards her her grin froze.

A moment later there was a blow to the back of his neck. Once he'd steadied himself he spun round and swore. The stable boy's face was twisted in fury. From his pocket he'd drawn a curved hoof pick.

Titus dropped his weight onto his back foot and raised his fists. The stable boy came at him, arm wheeling, and Titus felt a little rush of air as the hook swiped less than an inch from his cheekbone. The boy was too angry to control himself and would not care if he took Titus's eye out.

Then something landed on the cobbles to his right. It was a carving knife. He risked a glance back to see Hannah standing in the doorway.

'He'll kill you otherwise!'

Titus put his foot on the handle of the knife and slid it back to her.

'He's not worth hanging for,' he said.

'Too scared for a proper fight,' the stable boy sneered.

'A proper fight is with your fists.'

The boy made a noise in his throat and then spat a gob of phlegm that struck Titus's shoulder. It stank of meat.

'If you hurt him I'll kill you!' Hannah cried.

The boy crept a few paces forward.

In a quick and fluid movement Titus kicked him hard in his upper arm and the hook clattered to the cobbles. But he was more agile than Titus had expected and immediately crouched and swept it up with his other hand. Titus sprang at him and managed to force his arm up his back. The boy cried out in pain but, before the fingers loosened on the hook, he flung himself forwards and his body weight threw them both onto the ground. Titus was pinned beneath him. He was so heavy Titus could barely breathe. With one arm pressed against Titus's throat the boy brought the hand holding the hook up between their bodies. Titus felt the tip of it gouge along his thigh towards his groin. The boy grinned at him.

'At least you won't be spawning any more vermin . . .'

Titus butted him in the face.

The boy's head snapped back and blood exploded from his nose. He tumbled back onto the cobbles to roll around, clutching his face and spluttering.

Titus got to his feet. His ribs were bruised and the inside of his left thigh was wet with blood. Even now the stable boy's feet wheeled, trying to trip him. Titus gave him one last kick between the legs and the boy was finally subdued, then he turned and hobbled back to the kitchen. But a larger shadow than Hannah's was now blocking out the light.

'WHAT IS THIS?' Inspector Pilbury roared.

'We had a disagreement,' Titus muttered.

'He attacked me, sir!' the stable boy sobbed, staggering up and holding out his bloody palms for the Inspector to see. 'He meant to kill me with that!'

He pointed a shaking finger at the knife still lying on the cobbles.

'It's not true,' Hannah cried. 'He started it and Titus was only protecting himself—'

'QUIET!' Pilbury bellowed.

Hannah's mouth snapped shut.

'You!' He jabbed a finger at the boy. 'Get back to the stable and prepare the carriage before I horsewhip you, and you . . .' his tone grew weary as he turned to Titus, 'take your sister home.'

Head bent, Titus shuffled past Pilbury into the kitchen. Hannah had started to cry and he put his arm around her. As they trudged out of the kitchen and along the corridor the policemen were emerging from the offices. Their ridged, bell-shaped helmets gave them an imposing appearance but their faces were anxious and several had taken the opportunity for a hasty pipe.

As they passed the front desk, heading for the open door, the sweet smell of tobacco was replaced by something more choking. Fingers of grey crept across the threshold.

'Smog,' Hannah said, wrinkling her nose.

'That's not smog,' the duty sergeant said, 'it's smoke. Coming up from the south-west by the look of it. Another fire in the Devil's Acre, I shouldn't wonder.'

As they stepped out onto King Street the prison cart

thundered past them. The sight of that black iron box made Titus's heart pound. He had accompanied his father here on one occasion in that coffin and the journey still haunted his dreams. The barred window was barely the size of a handkerchief and when the door clanged shut upon them and the driver whipped up the horses Titus had almost fainted with terror. It was like being transported through hell. The total darkness, the thundering of the road through the iron walls, the violent shaking of the whole and the urine-stench of fear was enough to send his father even madder: he had thrashed like a wild animal and broken his son's nose.

The cobbles reopened a cut in his foot. Until last year he had owned a pair of shoes, paid for by their mother's dressmaking, back when she sewed until one or two in the morning instead of sleeping off drink, but they were long ago sold. Most Acre children went barefoot, and soon their soles were so tough that a steel tack could barely pierce them.

At the corner Titus turned back for one last look at the police station. He'd been determined to prove to Pilbury that he was more than just a wretched street brat destined for drink, crime and the gallows, but the fight with the stable boy had ruined everything. Titus had shown himself to be the same as all the rest.

And now they were heading back where they belonged.

They crossed Victoria Street, dodging the mounds of horse dung and the carriages that swirled up out of the grey, before finally passing into the environs of the Devil's Acre.

# 4

# CHEAP THRILLS

The darkness seemed even deeper after the glitz of Victoria Street and the smoke grew thicker at every step. They picked their way slowly down Abbey Orchard Street and into Perkins Rents. This wider street made a tunnel for the wind and the smoke cleared enough for them to see a few feet in front of them. Just in time Titus managed to avoid treading on a broken bottle sticking up from the mud.

A rustle to their left made him stop dead and thrust Hannah behind him.

'Evening, Titus. And how's my little darlin', then?'

The voice from the shadows was very familiar.

'Evening, Stitcher.'

A boy with soot-black hair jumped onto the tumble-down wall next to them. The halo of gold bobbing along the other side of the wall must be Charly. Charly was so fair that people who saw him and Hannah together took them for siblings. Titus's own hair was blond (when it was clean enough to tell), but nowhere near as fair as Hannah's.

'Found your way home all right, then?' Stitcher said to Hannah. 'Only we was worried as we left in a bit of a hurry, what with Charly's dicky tum. River mud always makes him heave. Did you find anything?'

Hannah glanced at Titus and bit her lip.

Stitcher jumped down from the wall and landed as nimbly as a cat in front of them. Though at least two heads shorter than Titus, Stitcher was fifteen too. Charly, who now climbed over to join them, was seven but as small as a toddler.

'Mudlarking again, were you?' Titus said.

'Yeh. Never find much these days though,' Stitcher said with a shrug. 'The water moves too quick now with the embankment and all.'

You had to admire Stitcher's attention to detail when it came to lying – it was entirely true that the recently completed embankment, built over the new sewer system, had narrowed and deepened the river's channel, making mudlarking even more dangerous.

Titus nodded in agreement, then added, 'And what with the tide being in all day.'

Stitcher cleared his throat a few times before continuing:

'Yeah, well, there is that bit of beach by the glass factory what's a bit higher than the rest and . . .'

'You wasn't mudlarking. I picked her up from the cop shop.'

'Well, that ain't nothing to do with me. We left her down by Westminster Bridge cos Charly had the shits.'

Titus stopped and turned to face the black-haired boy.

'You wanna muck up your own life, Stitch, go ahead, but if you try and take Hannah with you, you'll have me to answer to.'

'You threatenin' me, mate?' Stitcher said, smiling amiably.

'I'm promising you,' Titus said.

For a moment they just stared at each other.

'You know what,' Stitcher said eventually, 'I miss you.'

Titus swallowed but held his gaze.

'It ain't as much fun without you.'

He reached forwards and laid a hand on Titus's shoulder.

'What are you tryin' to prove? That you're clever? We all know that. That you're better than us; that you're one of them? You think they're gonna let you escape from this place?' He swung his arm round, taking in the soot-stained walls, the rags at the windows. 'Go ahead and try it. You go earn a penny a month in the tanners' yards or the shipyards or the sewers. And when she grows up Hannah can bloody her fingers making dresses for rich tarts, or get phossy jaw in the match factories. Or there's always whoring, until she's too old or too rotten.'

Seeing Titus's expression Stitcher held his hands up in supplication.

'It's only the truth. Why don't you just let her enjoy herself while she's young enough to get away with it, eh? Your mate on the force ain't gonna let her get into too much trouble, is he?'

'Leave her alone, Stitcher,' Titus said quietly. 'I mean it.'

'Or else what?'

But before Titus could reply Charly leaped in front of him and started skipping and dancing in such a peculiar fashion that Titus couldn't help laughing. A moment later the child had vanished and Stitcher was up on the wall again. In his fingers glinted the Inspector's penny.

'In these parts you gotta know what side your bread's buttered!' he crowed, then tossed the coin up in the air, caught it deftly and vanished over the wall. 'Be seeing you, Tight-Arse!'

Titus swore loudly and would have gone after him, but Stitcher knew these streets even better than he did. His cackles rebounded off the walls and cobbles long after the boys vanished into the swirling grey.

'Come on,' Titus snapped and for once Hannah did as she was told.

As they pressed further into the maze of alleys, the cobbles gave way to mud and worse. The air was now so thick with smoke they almost missed the turning to their street. When they did find it, the way was blocked by a throng of people. Above their heads Titus could see orange flames licking the black sky. It was the house opposite theirs: he recognised it by the elaborate brick chimney, the only one in the street that hadn't fallen down.

Luckily for this landlord the pump was on the next street and the house was so overcrowded that there were at least forty people who had an interest in dousing the flames. As he pushed through the jostling backs, Titus recognised the smut-blackened faces of the children from the window opposite theirs. One of them clutched a clumsy wooden doll, naked but for a scarlet ribbon in its wool hair.

''Ere, that ain't your blanket,' someone said loudly.

A large, red-faced man was squaring up to the skinny father of the child with the doll.

'Yes it is,' the smaller man snapped, bundling the blanket to his wife. 'I saved it from the fire meself.'

'Like hell you did! You half-inched it on your way down. Now, give it back if you know what's good for you,' and he smacked the skinny man on the shoulder, sending him staggering into his wife. She thrust him forwards, bawling, 'Don't give it him, Jonas!'

The red-faced man took so long drawing back his fist that Jonas had time to aim a sharp kick at his balls. There were loud 'oohs' from the crowd as their attention turned away from the fire and onto the fight. Only Jonas's daughter seemed uninterested in her father's fate. She was staring directly upwards. She said something: it was impossible to hear over the din of the fight but Titus thought it might have been 'bird'.

He followed her gaze.

A single long tongue of flame was stretching out from the burning house to lick the rag flapping at Titus and Hannah's window. The rag, greasy with dirt and dry after a few days without rain, caught immediately.

Titus thrust his way through the crowd to the door of the house where his landlords, Mr and Mrs Pincher, stood grinning as they watched the fight.

'Look!' he screamed, jabbing his finger into the air. Their grins froze as they followed the line of it. They all saw the burning rag tear free of the window frame and waft inside the building. Titus forced them out of his way and took the stairs two at a time.

By the time he made the third floor, acrid smoke was tumbling down the stairs. The fire must have caught his mother's workpile by the window. She had fallen so behind that the stack of garments for mending and alterations had grown almost as tall as Hannah.

Bursting out onto the top landing he flung himself into the burning room.

The heat was incredible: it distorted the air into rippling spectres that streamed towards him and seared his hair. There was so much smoke, billowing like ink in water. The source of the smoke was the bed. His father slept nearest the window and would be in the most imminent danger if the mattress was on fire.

'Wake up, Mother!' he screamed as he found his father's legs and dragged him off the bed. Crouching beneath the smoke Titus could see that his father was not burned at all, though his eyes were closed and his face was pale. Titus dragged him out of the room then plunged back into the inferno. The heat had intensified and it was now accompanied by a smell that it took Titus some moments to recognise. When he did so, he let out a cry of horror and flung himself at the black maelstrom that had been the bed.

Through the smoke he could see flutters of red. His mother's hair and right arm were on fire. Bellowing for her to wake up, he batted blindly at the flames then heaved her onto his shoulder. Though she was as light as a child, the mattress was collapsing beneath him and every movement was like wading through tar. All around him the room groaned and shrieked.

And then he felt her arm tighten around his neck.

'Mother!' he screamed.

She murmured something into his ear and he was sure he felt, amidst the rush of searing wind and the rain of soot, the brush of her lips on his cheek.

Smoke had clogged his lungs and as he tried to take a breath he was overcome with coughing. At every gasp between coughs his lungs seized up more and he grew weaker.

He fell to his knees and just managed to drag them both out of the room onto the landing before collapsing. As he lay gulping down the cool air coming up the stairs he heard voices and footsteps.

Two boys appeared on the landing, carrying a tin bath. They hobbled along as fast as they could with their awkward load, slopping water as they went, and paused in the doorway to the burning room.

'Chuck it straight in, then go down for more!'

He knew the voice but his vision was blurred and his eyeballs scraped against his dry lids.

Then someone knelt beside him.

'Come on, mate. Get up now, you can do it.'

As he struggled into a sitting position he heard the slosh of water followed by a furious hiss.

'Go on, then, go back! And make room for the boys coming up!'

Titus rubbed his eyes and opened them. The two boys scurried past and down the stairs just as a second pair emerged on the landing, with another tin bath – this one pouring water from several rust holes.

'We carried your dad outside, now let's get your ma down.'

The boy had his mother under the arm. His black hair was pasted to his forehead with sweat and runnels of dirt poured down his neck.

'Stitcher?'

'Come on. She needs air.'

Titus stood and wrapped her other arm around his neck and the two boys staggered down the stairs.

But his mother needed more than just air. Even as one

of the navvies crouched over her, his mouth clamped over hers, forcing his own breath into her motionless chest, Titus knew it was useless. It must have been the smoke. At least she hadn't burned to death. Hannah clung to her mother, pressing her head into her parent's stomach, her screams muffled by the burned rags of her dress.

Titus went over to where his father lay, his face covered by someone's silk handkerchief.

'There weren't nothing to be done,' someone said. 'His heart must have given out.'

Titus knelt down and took his father's hand. It was still warm. The line of a purple scar ran horizontally across his palm: from the time his father had taken hold of a bayonet blade as its Russian owner tried to thrust it into the wounded body of one of his friends. This was the only story his father ever told about the war, and only because Hannah kept plaguing him about the scar.

Titus laid the hand palm down on his father's chest and then placed the other over it.

A couple of women from the street were crouching beside Hannah, murmuring words of comfort. One old lady he didn't recognise was holding his mother's hand, patting and stroking it and holding it to her sunken cheek.

An hour too late a little red fire engine finally arrived and several burly men jumped down and began violently pumping their water apparatus. Within a few minutes the flames were out and the street became gloomy once more. Most of the onlookers began to disperse.

And then, in a dying flare from one of the upper storeys, a flash of gold near his mother's hand caught Titus's eye.

The old woman's gimlet gaze met his as her bony fingers closed over his mother's wedding ring.

'Hey!' he shouted, lunging at her.

Suddenly she threw herself backwards onto the cobbles, clutching her face.

'Oh, oh, oh!' she howled. 'He hit me! He hit me!'

One of the firemen ran over and helped her to her feet.

'Who did it, lady?'

'Him, there! The skinny one!'

She pointed a shaking finger with Titus's mother's ring glimmering on it.

# 5

# THE PRISONER

The cell was narrow, damp and ice-cold. Its whitewashed walls were windowless but a small barred aperture in the door looked onto the courtyard. The only furniture was a rectangular wooden block to be used as a bed.

For some time after he'd been thrown in, Titus could do nothing but huddle shivering on the bed with his face to the wall and his arms wrapped tightly around his knees. They had been rough with him because he hadn't gone quietly. He'd tried to talk to Hannah who was screaming as one of the other firemen restrained her. He'd wanted to tell her to go back into the house and wait for him. He asked the fireman holding him to let him go back and speak to her, that their parents had both died, but all he got was a punch in the stomach which made it impossible to say any more.

Eventually the pains in his stomach eased and he rolled onto his back and straightened out, staring up at the cracks in the ceiling. After a few minutes, Big Ben struck one. Everything was silent. Had all the policemen gone home? They'd told him nothing when they put him in here. The duty officer seemed distracted, almost forgetting to lock the cell, then hurrying away directly afterwards.

He was thirsty but the jug that sat in a bowl in the corner was empty.

What were he and Hannah going to do now?

Shame engulfed him. He'd wasted all that time at the Ragged School to try and 'better himself', but if he'd brought in just a few more pennies then there might have been enough food to go round. He had tried. When he was twelve he'd gone round the markets asking for work, but when they found out where he lived they didn't want to know. Only dirty thieves lived in the Acre. Perhaps the only sensible option left was crime. Why didn't he get his thumb out of his backside, throw in his lot with Stitcher again?

A sudden commotion from the courtyard made him get up and go over to the window. The stable lad, the one he'd fought with, held open the gates for the prison cart and as it hurtled through the men on top yelled at him to close it as quickly as he could.

The cart came to a standstill in the middle of the yard and the men tumbled off it as if it were red-hot. There were at least six of them and for a moment they stood in little groups muttering to one another. The stable boy fastened the gates and then came over to stand with them.

Inside the cart someone started singing. As the reedy falsetto drifted through the night air the policemen fell silent.

'Is that what yer all scared of?' the stable boy jeered. 'Some drunk old tart?'

The singing stopped abruptly. The stable boy carried his lantern up to the cart and rapped on the metal side.

'All right, darlin'? Fancy a quickie?'

For a moment there was silence. The stable boy pressed his ear to the metal.

'Hello . . . o . . . o . . . o . . .!'

One of the policemen hushed him but the stable boy ignored him and opened his mouth to speak again. There was an almighty bang and the lantern went sailing through the air. From the prison cart there came a cacophony of barking and snarling, as if it was filled with a hundred crazed pit bull terriers. The lantern exploded against the station wall in a fireball which momentarily lit up the darkness. The image of the stable boy frozen in mid-air was seared into Titus's vision before the courtyard went black.

In the darkness that followed all that could be heard were the stable boy's yelps and a low guttural laughing.

More lanterns were brought from inside the station, and more men. They trooped past Titus's cell, their faces pale. The last to emerge was Inspector Pilbury. As they joined in a wide circle around the cart each man drew his truncheon.

Pilbury walked around the back.

'Rancer!'

His voice rang through the courtyard.

'I have ten armed men ready to bring you down if you put up a struggle. I myself have a pistol. When I open these doors you will come quietly or you will suffer for it.'

The key snicked in the lock and the black door of the cart swung out. Inspector Pilbury took a step back and drew his pistol.

'Get out,' he said quietly.

Then there came a child's voice:

'Let me go, please! My father's rich, he'll pay you whatever you ask, I won't say who you are I swear.' The child began to giggle, and then the giggle became deeper and deeper until it was that mocking, guttural laugh again.

Pilbury raised his lantern higher. The shadows in front of him began to blacken and congeal until finally they formed themselves into the figure of a man.

'Mr Pilbury, sir, are you quite well?'

'You know my name,' Pilbury said evenly, though he had to tip back his head to address the prisoner. 'You are not quite the madman, then?'

He did not take his eyes from the hulk as he called to his men:

'Jackson, see to the boy. Samson, Harris and the rest of you, take him to cell three. I want to be able to see him from my office.'

He waited until four officers had cuffed themselves to the prisoner before walking rapidly away towards the kitchen. As soon as he had disappeared into the building the prisoner began to struggle. Two of the men were knocked to the floor immediately and more piled on to replace them until they became a heaving mountain of fists and boots and truncheons.

What with all the scuffling, the curses from the officers and the bellowing of their prisoner, Titus was so distracted that it took some moments for him to notice the figures standing in the window opposite the cells.

One was Inspector Pilbury. A little further back from him stood the top-hatted master of ceremonies from the Palace Theatre, his face set into a scowl. Next to Pilbury stood the medium. Tonight she was wearing a pale blue dress: judging by the way the fabric gathered under the sash around her waist he guessed it was several sizes too big for her. He recognised her by her fine black hair but without this it would have been almost impossible, because something strange had happened to her features. Her eyes had widened, and something in the way the light fell on her face made it seem more rounded, childlike almost. Her delicate hands clutched what looked like a rag doll. Her gaze was fixed on the passage of the felon and as the thrashing body disappeared into the cell Titus saw Pilbury murmur something into her ear. She gave a slow and deliberate nod then slumped into the Inspector's arms.

When she stood up again it was with the distracted air of someone woken from a dream. Her features were now as Titus remembered them from the séance, and she turned and spoke anxiously to the policeman. Pilbury's reply made her bury her face in her hands. The policeman vanished and returned with a blanket, which he wrapped carefully about her shoulders, and led her from the room. The top-hatted man, his expression still sour, turned and followed them out.

Titus pressed his cheek to the bars of his door and watched the officers emerge from cell three. After locking the door they slammed shut the metal hatch that covered the bars, but it didn't silence the noise from inside. Though all the officers had withdrawn to the courtyard it sounded as if cell three was filled with a hundred people: Titus could hear a baby crying, women giggling, a songbird chirruping the very same tune their own poor bird had sung, and over it all the voice of the prisoner bellowing the Inspector's name.

The men walked quickly to the far end of the courtyard and leaned against the wall for a pipe. Each one held his lantern close and the orange light shivered, casting jittery shadows on the stable walls. One had a bloodied nose and even from here Titus could see that the hands tamping down the tobacco were shaking. The stable boy was helped out of the gates sobbing that his ribs were broken.

After their pipes the men dispersed. Some went out of the gates, some back inside the station. Gradually the lamps went out until only Pilbury's and the kitchen's remained lit. Cell three eventually fell silent.

Big Ben struck two.

Titus went back and sat down on the bed and wondered how Hannah was. If she had been taken back to Stitcher's at least she'd have Rosie to comfort her. If she'd done as she was told and stayed with the Pinchers she'd be shivering on a hard floor, alone and scared, weeping in the darkness. He was a fool to have told her to remain.

A noise outside brought him back to the window. Perhaps the duty officer was coming to release him.

Inspector Pilbury stood in the moonlight in the middle of the courtyard. A match flared, illuminating his tired face, and then the sweet pipe smoke drifted across in a silver ribbon to Titus's cell. Titus let him enjoy the pipe for a few minutes before calling quietly:

"Scuse me, Mr Pilbury? Can you tell me how long I'm likely to be here? It's just that Hannah's all alone and . . .'

'Titus?'

The Inspector came over and squinted into the darkness.

'What are you doing here? It's not like you to get yourself into bother.'

'My parents . . .' His voice faltered under Pilbury's kindly gaze. 'My parents are dead. There was a fire. An old woman tried to steal Mother's wedding ring off her finger and when I tried to get it back she said I'd struck her.'

The Inspector gave a long sigh.

'Where's Hannah?'

'Back at the house I hope.'

Pilbury tapped his pipe against the wall and tucked it back into his pocket.

'I'll go and speak to the duty officer.'

He set off in the direction of the main building and a few minutes later came back with the keys.

'The old woman never turned up to press charges so you're free to go.'

'Thank you, sir.'

'I'll let you out the back gate.'

As they walked down the line of cells a soprano's voice trilled.

'P . . . i . . . l . . . berrrrr . . . y . . . y . . . y . . . y . . . y . . . y!'

Pilbury's truncheon flew out and the door of cell three gave a dull clang that reverberated around the courtyard. The opera singer began to sob theatrically.

When they'd got a safe distance away Titus muttered: 'Who is that?'

Pilbury paused by the stable and clicked his tongue into the darkness. A few minutes later a grey horse trotted up. Its head was high and the whites of its eyes were visible around the large brown iris.

'She looks scared,' Titus said.

'She's every right to be,' the Inspector murmured, running the back of his hand down the animal's nose. 'Have you heard of the Wigman?'

Titus nodded. 'Course. He's been killing slum kids all summer. Taking a bit of their hair as a souvenir.'

'Yes. That is one of his trademarks. There are others the press haven't been told about, to prevent all the local lunatics wasting our time with their confessions.'

'Is it him in there?' Titus whispered, jerking his thumb back towards cell three. Pilbury nodded.

Titus threw a glance over his shoulder at the black metal door of cell three. He wasn't superstitious but it had been hard not to be affected by some of the stories whirling around the Acre: that the devil himself was stalking them, to punish them for their sinful deeds.

'How did you catch him?' he said.

'He left footprints on the riverbank and a doctor of anatomy told us their owner must be at least six feet. A giant like that stands out in the Acre.'

Titus nodded, but he couldn't help wondering about the medium at the window.

'He sounds mad,' Titus said. 'Will he escape the gallows because of it?'

'I believe the madness is affected for that end. I don't like sending any man to be hanged but this one . . .' He tailed off. Digging his hand into his pocket he brought out a saffron bun, which the horse gobbled gratefully.

'I didn't realise buns was part of your kit, sir,' Titus said.

Pilbury smiled. 'My old housekeeper will insist on trying to feed me up. The house is heaving with pies and cakes and bloody buns. Would you like me to bring some in for you?'

'That's very kind of you, sir, but I'm sure we'll manage.'

'Very well,' Pilbury said, then he laid a hand lightly on Titus's shoulder. 'But is there nothing I can do to help you both?'

Titus cleared his throat and looked away before replying:

'Perhaps a few buns then, if you can spare them. For Hannah.'

'Of course.'

They walked together to the gate and said goodnight.

# 6

# THE BASEMENT

He hammered on the door until Mr and Mrs Pincher finally came down.

'Is she here?'

The dancing candle flame contorted their features, throwing shadows of beaks and claws against the wall behind them.

'Did you think we would throw a poor orphan out into the street?' Mrs Pincher said.

He barged past them into the hallway and began mounting the stairs to their old apartment.

'Not that way!' the old woman called.

He came back and followed them down the hall to the cellar door. As they descended the stairs into the cellar Mr Pincher told Titus how they had struggled to get the bodies inside:

'We wanted to do right by them, for we were so fond of your poor dear mother.'

Titus's jaw clenched. They had called his mother a drunken slut on more than one occasion.

As they neared the bottom there was a strong smell of earth and rats' urine. Mr Pincher stepped out onto the mud floor and held up the candle. Along the wall on the opposite side were two shrouded bodies. Titus took a step towards them. His mother's hand protruded from beneath the sheet, a depression in the flesh marking where the ring had been. Already her skin was waxy yellow. He knelt and tucked the hand back under the sheet.

They had misunderstood him, thinking he wanted to know where his parents were. Still, it was kind of the old buggers to have given them somewhere to be at peace. Hannah must be at Stitcher's.

But as he stood up a movement from the other side of the room caught his eye. Hannah was curled on a wooden pallet in the corner. Though it was freezing cold and damp she had no covering, nor any pillow. She did not register his presence but stared in the direction of the corpses, ceaselessly rubbing at her lips with her fist. Titus turned on the old couple who shrank back up the stairs.

'You forced her to stay with their bodies?'

'There was nowhere else!'

'There was your own lodgings.'

His mouth curled in disgust as they sighed and mumbled and wouldn't meet his gaze. Then a frail voice called his name.

'It's all right,' he said, turning back and sinking to his knees beside her, 'I'm here now.'

He took her in his arms and embraced her while she whimpered, stroking her hair and murmuring words of comfort. Eventually she fell asleep and he laid her carefully back onto the pallet, with his own jumper as a pillow. When he looked back at the stairs his landlords had vanished, leaving the guttering candle on the stairs. Exhaustion finally overcame him and he lay down on the mud next to her, on his side to create a wall between her and what lay beyond.

When he woke she was staring up at the ceiling. A little morning light came down the stairs from the open door at the top, and coloured her face a sickly yellow. His father always said her eyes were as blue as cornflowers, but in the light of that cold morning they were the opaque green of stagnant water.

Mrs Pincher was good enough to let Hannah wait in her kitchen while Titus did his best to clean up the room. It wasn't as bad as it had appeared when the fire raged: only the most flammable items – the linen, the straw mattress and bedframe – had burned, while the roof and walls were only scorched and stained with soot. They would have to sleep on the bare cot until he found the money to replace the linen. Where that was to come from he had no idea. There was no sense trying to maintain the dressmaking business. Besides the destruction of all the work waiting to be done, his mother had an excellent reputation, built up before her marriage, and no-one would trust a cack-handed boy and his little sister to produce work of the same quality. Little did they know that their fine dresses had been produced by just such a pair for the past year.

At ten the men arrived to take their parents' remains to the paupers' burial ground at St Bride's. They were quiet and respectful and when Titus asked the time of the funeral service they told him gently that there would be a mass burial at four that afternoon, in a communal pit.

'The air is not so sweet, and the preacher not so devout as you would wish, son,' said the older man with a sad smile. 'Why not simply say a prayer and drop a flower into the river? God will hear you.' When he placed his wiry hand on Titus's shoulder Titus almost crumpled with the safety and strength of it. Before he climbed up onto the cart the younger man reached beneath the shroud and snipped off a lock of his mother's chestnut hair. 'Here,' he said, 'remember her as she was.'

The sun was beginning to set when he descended the stairs for the final time, the bucket slopping black water over his trousers. He had changed it six times, trekking to the pump on the corner of the street, ignoring the curious eyes and shouts of the street children. Stitcher made a brief appearance to slap some of the younger ones about the ears until they fled crying, before telling Titus how sorry he was.

'I can't remember nothing about my folks, though Rosie says when they found me I was wearing a silver locket. Someone pinched that soon enough, course. Never mind. Me and Charly got each other at least.'

He nodded up at Mrs Pincher's window: 'I could give them two a hiding for you if you like.'

'That's all right,' Titus said. 'Thanks anyway.'

He went back up for a final check of the room before Hannah came up. Even now, after a good clean, it was a grim and depressing hole. Its shape may once have been square, but age had bowed it, so that on one side the wall lurched inwards, and on the other it leaned drunkenly away. Mildew spread up the walls and across the ceiling, making it feel as if the room was in the middle of a dark wood.

The only furniture left in the room was the bare cot and

the poor little songbird's cage. Hannah always wanted to set it free, imagining her own love for the bird was reciprocated strongly enough for it to return of its own free will, but Titus knew it would have been out of the window in a heartbeat and set upon by gulls or crows. A kinder death, perhaps. Despite passing so close to it the flames had left the cage almost untouched, although the brass was now black, but the heat and smoke must have been too much for the little creature. He took it from the cage and, with nowhere else to put it, slipped the frail body into his pocket. Then he made his way downstairs.

Hannah was staring out of the window while Mrs Pincher pored over her ledger. On a plate next to it was a half-eaten pie, and she was smearing its grease over the pages as she wrote.

'Come on, Hannah, time to go back up.'

The scratch of Mrs Pincher's pen paused.

'Back up?' she said.

'To the room. I've cleaned it and it's now habitable.'

'Oh no, son.' She bent her thin lips into an innocent smile. 'The room is taken.'

'What?'

'Yes. By the poor family who lost their home yesterday.'

She laughed at the expression on Titus's face.

'What, d'you think I'd be letting it out for free to a couple of guttersnipes without a bean between them?'

For a moment he couldn't speak. It was Hannah who finally broke the silence.

'You let him do all that work knowing you was gonna throw us out?' she said.

'Your parents were dead drunk.' Her smile drew as fine as wire. 'If they'd been sober they would have got up and put out them first little flames and there would have been no damage to the room.'

Titus stared at her. She swallowed a piece of pie crust and the little lump moved down her scrawny throat to be lost amidst the brown folds. Her neck was as thin as a chicken leg. His hands clenched into fists at his side.

Then Hannah's fingers wormed into his.

'Come on,' she said quietly. 'We'll go to Stitcher's place.'

'That's it,' the old woman mumured. 'Birds of a feather . . .'

Titus inhaled deeply, then cleared his throat.

'Perhaps you would consider letting us stay this one night, as it is too late to organise alternative lodgings.'

'I told you the room is already taken.'

'Is there not a hallway or storeroom we might use. I should pay you back of course, once I am salaried.'

She laughed.

'Oh, of course. I hear all the businesses are clamouring to hire illiterate orphans.'

'I can read and write. I learned at the One Tun School.'

'Oh yes, Ragged Schools are famous for producing millionaires,' she tittered, returning to the ledger. 'Well, when you are *salaried* you will be more than welcome.'

They were supposed to leave now but, despite his revulsion for the landlady and his shame at having to beg, he stayed where he was. He owed Hannah at least one more attempt.

'If you will not help us, just for this one night, then we will have nowhere to go.'

'There's always the workhouse.'

He flinched. Then he took Hannah's hand and led her to the door. If they had any chance of securing beds for the night they must leave now. The pawnshop two streets away might give them a few pence for Hannah's coat.

'Wait a minute, my dear.'

Mr Pincher's voice wheedled from the corner of the room where Titus now saw him, curled on his overstuffed armchair like a spider feeding on a fat fly.

'What about the basement room?'

Mrs Pincher blinked at him.

'The cellar?'

'No, my sweet,' he stared at his wife with bulbous grey eyes, 'I mean the basement.'

Comprehension spread across her face like syrup.

'For some time we have been planning to renovate downstairs and although, as you have seen, it is not quite ready for immediate habitation, perhaps we could hold it for you, for the price of, say, tuppence a week, until such time as that amounts to a month's deposit.'

'We'll sleep there tonight, if you have another pallet, and I'll get you the deposit as soon as I can.'

'No!' Hannah cried.

'We have no choice!' he hissed at her.

'No deposit, no room,' Mrs Pincher sing-songed, returning to her ledger.

It didn't look like the old bag could be persuaded. But in the long run it might be worth keeping on the right side of them. Tuppence a week was very cheap, especially if they were going to do up the place. And if Titus managed to find work he might scrape the deposit together quite quickly.

'You will do what needs to be done quickly? The walls must be painted and a floor laid.'

'Oh I agree, the walls do need painting,' Mr Pincher said, 'and a wooden floor should certainly be laid if it is to be comfortable.'

'Tuppence a week?'

The old man nodded, smiling.

'Then hold it for us and I will be back with the deposit as soon as I can.'

He leaned forwards and shook Mrs Pincher's hand, holding her gaze with a confidence he did not feel. Despite the grease and clumps of meat under her nails it was like holding a bag of sticks. Hannah leaned heavily against him, her breath soured by fatigue and hunger.

'To seal our arrangement,' he said, 'perhaps you might share with us a little of that meat pie.'

Mrs Pincher threw back her head, stretching taut the sinews of her neck.

'The boy is a chancer!' she cried. 'Here!'

She tossed over the grey lump and then licked the fat from her fingers.

Hannah munched her way solidly through the pie as they passed out of the streets of the Acre into Victoria Street. All hunger had left him, however, and his throat was bone dry.

What he was about to do, the plan that might save them, meant betraying the last person in the world he had left to love.

# 7

# THE WORKHOUSE

To delay the moment he took a meandering route, eastwards towards the Houses of Parliament. Hannah soon realised that they were not going to Stitcher's.

'We must spend the night at the workhouse,' he told her.

'What? No! I'd rather die!'

'Just for the night. Tomorrow I'll find work and get us some lodgings.' He could barely shape his lips to form the treacherous words. 'You can manage one night, can't you?'

'Why can't we just go to Stitcher's?'

Because, he wanted to say, we will never come out again. Because it would be as easy as breathing to slip into his old ways again. Because they would both be happy for a while: amongst friends, with enough to eat and drink, warmth and comfort. Because he was beginning to wonder why he ever thought it wrong.

'Because I don't want to live like that any more. Please, just trust me.'

After he'd spoken he bit his cheek hard enough to draw blood.

The river was as busy as ever and people streamed across the bridge from Lambeth. On their right the Palace of Westminster raked the sky, leaving wheals of scarlet in the grey. Inside those walls MPs would be dining on mutton and gravy, plum pudding and custard, Stilton cheese. They would sup champagne, claret, port and brandy, and then topple groaning onto the pavement where their drivers waited to whisk them back to Belgravia. He understood what drove Stitcher and his crew to rob and terrorise with such indifference to their victims when they could be so warm and loyal to their friends. Stitcher and Titus and their kind were nearer to dogs than they were to the men who paced those hallowed halls. Their concerns were of simple animal survival, where these people existed in a world where the stitching on one's hat was a matter of life and death. A single gold button from their waistcoats would keep Titus and Hannah in food and lodgings for a week.

The tide was coming in and the water surged onto the beach below. Soon it would be submerged, but this was no deterrent to the mudlark who delved in the last few inches of sludge in front of them, occasionally plucking some-thing out, wiping it on her smock and pocketing it. The current was strong enough to snatch her away if she did not leave soon, but her survival was just as dependent on the mud of the riverbed.

Was survival worth so much pain?

He gazed down at the water. A quick release for himself, and quicker for Hannah, who would have no warning and so no fear. Then he felt something pressing against his hip and drew from his pocket the body of the songbird. His body heat had kept the little thing warm and supple, and its tissue-thin eyelids were closed, as if it were only sleeping. The sun broke through the clouds as he hurled it out across the river and it arced down like a falling star. As it drew near to the surface of the water the wind caught its wings and threw them wide. This slowed its fall momentarily, but then there was some convulsion in the little body and, even as the waves stretched their fingers to receive it, the bird bobbed, hovered and rose up. Had a gust of wind decided to tease it a little before tossing it away? But now it was flying against the wind; diving forwards, soaring. Its head was raised and, even over the wind and the thunder of carriages, it was possible to hear its song.

Titus laughed with exhilaration. The mudlark, too, had witnessed this resurrection and stood transfixed as the bird tumbled through the air. Hannah finally stirred and her hair flashed in the sunlight, yellow as the bird's feathers, as she turned to follow Titus's gaze.

'See, Hannah! I have set her free! I have done it!'

They kept sight of the speck of gold until the river bent southwards.

'Course she'll be gobbled up by the crows,' the mudlark called, picking her way back up the now inundated beach, but her voice was bright.

For a few minutes his heart was light, watching Hannah squint into the distance for one last glimpse of the bird, but as the lower edge of the sun came to rest on Chelsea Bridge he knew it was time to continue their journey, into the gloomy alleys of Little Almonry.

The Westminster Workhouse was a three-storey, red-bricked building taking up over half an acre of land between the cathedral and the river. Its windows were tiny, like the scars on the face of a smallpox victim.

Titus and Hannah stood on the pavement, in front of an arch in the outer wall that led into a dreary courtyard. After the excitement of the songbird Hannah had lapsed back into listless silence, her head bent.

Through the arch came a biting north wind that tore around the courtyard and whipped at the clothes of those queuing for admittance. Beginning at a door on the far side the queue snaked all the way around the wall, under the arch and out here onto the pavement. Though there was a great diversity in those hoping for a bed – old, young, male, female, crippled, able-bodied, respectably dressed and filthily ragged – all were united in silence. The only sound was a monotonous clanging that came from the darkest corner of the yard, where men chipped at boulders with hammers.

They joined the end of the queue.

By the time they neared the front, the stonebreakers had been summoned away and the sun had fallen behind the building. The only light came from the glowing bowls of pipes in the queue behind him and the dim candlelight in the windows surrounding the courtyard. Shadows passed slowly behind the glass and there was a faint murmur of prayers.

Hannah had fallen into a doze against his shoulder and he moved carefully, so as not to wake her. They were third in line when the door burst open and a young woman was thrust out onto the courtyard.

'I am not drunk,' she cried. 'It's just that my legs is so cold they won't work properly!'

The door slammed shut.

'Bastard!' she shrieked, but after a moment her defiant

stance slumped and she began to weep. As the door opened to admit the next pauper the woman turned and walked, perfectly steadily, back out of the archway.

Though good sense told Titus it was a good thing that even the suspicion of drunkenness was enough to exclude a person, his heart shrank at such callousness and he clung more tightly to Hannah.

Now they were second in line. Panic rose in his gullet. Was this place as bad as they said: where starving paupers fought one another for the rotting marrow from bones they were supposed to be crushing? Where the newborn babies of unmarried mothers were sold into slavery? Where children who answered back had their tongues branded with an 'I' for Insolent? He had scoffed at Stitcher's wide-eyed tales, but here in this shivering darkness they seemed all too plausible.

The door opened and the next pauper was summoned. Behind him a woman was telling her two children that, whilst they would not be allowed to see one another, she would be thinking of them every moment. 'Look out at the moon tonight,' she said in a soft Irish accent, 'and I'll look out too, and in that way we shall be together.' The youngest child began to cry.

Titus stared at the door. Minutes passed. Hannah's heartbeat was slow and steady against his shoulder. He was surprised the wild leaping of his own did not shake her awake.

'Next!' roared a voice as heavy as a sledgehammer.

Titus pushed open the door and a blast of chill air ruffled Hannah's hair. He half carried her through and it banged shut behind him. The sudden change in atmosphere woke her and she looked around, wide-eyed.

Behind a desk in front of them a face as cold and round as the moon's glowed in the light of a candle.

'Name.'

'Titus Adams.'

'Age.'

'It's not me. It's my sister. I wish to give you my sister.'

'What?' Hannah said.

'Name.'

'Her name is Hannah Adams.'

'Age.'

'Nine.'

'What?' Her voice rose in pitch. 'You said both of us!'

He stared resolutely in front of him as the man recorded her details.

'Titus!' She tried to pull his face around.

Several small huddles of people were gathered in different corners of the room. A door he had not noticed opened behind the moon-face and a young man appeared.

'Able-bodied Men Under Sixty!' he barked, and one of the groups detached itself from the corner and followed him out.

'Grounds for admission?' the moon-face snapped.

He was in his fifties, large-framed and strong-looking.

'Our parents have recently died and we have nowhere to go. As soon as I have gained employment I will be back to collect her.'

'Don't leave me here!' Hannah shrieked, tearing herself away from him.

'It won't be for long . . .'

'NO!'

She backed away then dived for the door. Titus caught her by the shoulder and muttered desperately:

'It's the only way. You will be here a matter of days, I swear!'

She twisted and lashed against his grasp, then he felt stronger arms than his take over.

The porter towered so far above him that Titus's nose was level with the chain of his pocket watch. With surprising gentleness he bent down to Hannah's level and held her arms to her sides. Immediately she grew still.

'Hush, my darling,' he said softly, 'you will come to no harm here.'

Her mouth trembled.

'Your brother has lied to you and forsaken you, but we will not.'

'Forsaken her?' Titus cried. 'You're the liar!'

A moment later he was flying backwards through the door, his skull cracking against the flagstones.

'Better the poor lamb be abandoned,' the porter roared, 'than grow up in the care of such a worthless piece of filth!'

Now Hannah was screaming, imprisoned by the porter's embrace but stretching her arms towards her brother.

'It's all right!' Titus cried over laughter and jeers from the other paupers. 'I'll be back for you soon. I swear!'

'The devil you will!' a voice cackled.

He scrambled to his feet and tried to reach his sister but the porter kicked him away. Now Hannah was writhing and spitting like a wild animal.

'Careful, my lovely!' the porter bellowed. 'Don't hurt yourself!'

'It's all right, Hannah! Everything will be all right!'

He would have tried to tear her from the porter's arms

if he thought he'd any chance, but now a young woman in a starched white apron came through the inner door. Hannah was bundled over to her, and the porter stood, an edifice of granite, between them.

'Get out, if you care at all for her distress.'

The nurse pressed Hannah's face to her bosom, muffling her screams. She managed to twist her head round and one wild eye, round as a calf's about to be slaughtered, stared from the folds of the woman's dress, before the door was slammed.

Titus lay where he was on the stones of the courtyard, as if every bone in his body was broken, until the last pauper had been devoured by the cold little room.

# 8

# EGGS AND HONEY

He read the note through one last time and winced at the now obvious spelling mistakes. He'd written it in a hurry on a scrap of newspaper for fear that the Inspector would have gone home. The words were crammed as neatly as possible into the blank space around an advertisement for face cream.

Dear Inspector Pilbury. I am writing this letter, though I cood ask in person, so as you can see that I can write middling well. I can also read and am a hard worker with no unsavery habits. I know that you are in need of a stableboy. I have had some expirience with horses at my grandmothers farm and was hoping you might consider me for the job.
Yours
sinserly,
Titus Adams

CRÊME de la

It would have to do.

The bell tinkled as he walked into the station but the duty officer was engrossed in his paper and didn't look up.

Titus cleared his throat.

The duty officer jumped as violently as if it had been a bomb going off.

'Good God, lad,' he puffed, laying his hand on his chest.

Titus apologised and slid the paper across the desk, blushing with shame as the duty officer picked it up with his fingertips, as if it were a soiled sock.

'It's a letter, sir,' he mumbled, 'for Inspector Pilbury.'

'The Inspector's very busy. Is it urgent?'

Titus nodded, avoiding his eye.

'Very well,' the man sighed. 'Wait here.'

Titus sat down on the bench. Somewhere in the distance a woman was singing a song Titus remembered from his babyhood, something to do with an apple and a worm.

Hannah would be in bed by now. Would she be sleeping? He doubted it. She would be cursing him and weeping and, if she'd continued to cause a commotion as they led her away, nursing the welts from a thrashing. He went over to the door and stared at his own reflection in the glass.

The singing had stopped, there was only the silence: oppressive and accusing.

The duty officer's paper still lay on the desk and, to distract his thoughts, Titus flicked back to the front page. It was about the prisoner he had seen arrive the previous night. The woodcut depicted a huge hairy beast swinging police officers around like rag dolls.

# WIGMAN CAGED

◆

Londoners can at last sleep peacefully in their beds tonight, safe in the knowledge that the city's worst childkiller has finally been apprehended.

Joseph Rancer, aged 28, was last night arrested at his home in the Westminster slum known as the 'Devil's Acre' and charged with all fifteen killings. He has been dubbed the Wigman after his penchant for stealing a lock of hair from each of his tiny victims, including the most recent, a boy of eight, whose body washed up on the beach beneath Westminster Bridge last week. All the victims were found in the river or washed up around the Westminster area. Though no motive has yet been offered for the crimes, the folk of the 'Devil's Acre' assert they were performed in the name of witchcraft. Rancer's mother was notorious in the area for her curious remedies, and woe betide those who brought down her wrath upon them: rumour has it that she murdered her husband.

The arrest must be a welcome relief for Police Inspector William Pilbury who has struggled with his own personal tragedy, which many believe may have affected his performance.

Rancer is to be tried within the month at the Old Bailey and will almost certainly hang. The evidence against him is strong - the hair of the victims has been found at his place of residence and his footprints were present at several of the crime scenes

'The Inspector will see you.'

The duty officer was holding open the internal door for him. Titus put down the paper and followed him up the corridor to the first office.

'Here he is, sir,' the officer said and pushed Titus through the door, closing it behind him. Pilbury did not look up from his writing but motioned for Titus to sit.

A copy of the *Standard* lay on the desk – Pilbury must have read the words questioning his ability. Next to it was a rusty tin, the lid half closed. A wisp of fair hair stuck out from under it.

Pilbury set down his pen.

'So,' he said, smiling wearily, 'you want a job.'

'Yes, sir.'

'Sit down, you look tired.'

'I am not. I have a great deal of stamina.'

Nevertheless he sank into the chair on the other side of the desk.

A commotion from the courtyard made Pilbury look behind him out of the window. The officer Titus recognised as Sergeant Samson was emerging from the stables, slapping his hands together to try and dislodge some of the hay that stuck to them. One of the other men stood in the courtyard waiting for him with a file of papers.

'For God's sake, man, can't you see I'm up to my eyes in horse shit?' Samson barked. The younger man stood his ground with admirable bravery.

'Samson has been minding the horses this week,' Pilbury said, 'but his wife is all in a tizzy over the early mornings and late nights. Go and find him and tell him you're the new stable boy. Just until the usual lad recovers, mark you.'

For a moment Titus just stared at him.

'Well, go on, lad, before I change my mind. And tell Samson to get you a pair of decent hobnail boots. You can't be paddling in horse piss all day with bare feet.'

Titus sprang from the chair, leaned over the desk and pumped the Inspector's hand until the older man laughed.

'Thank you!' he panted, then bolted for the door. Halfway down the corridor Titus stopped, ran back and poked his head through the door.

'When will I be paid?'

Without lifting his eyes from his paperwork, Pilbury said, 'End of the month, like everyone else,' but then his pen paused and he looked up. 'Hannah's well, I trust?'

'Oh, very well,' Titus said breezily, 'she's staying with a relative in the country.'

Pilbury nodded and smiled. 'Excellent.'

Titus turned and sped off in the direction of the stables before Pilbury could notice he was blushing.

If Samson was pleased to see him he didn't show it.

''Bout bloody time,' he snapped as he swept horse dung into a steaming pile in the corner of the yard.

'The market boys'll be round for that tomorrow. Now, what do you know about horses?'

The animals were called Leopold and Beatrice. They were both friendly, though rather skittish, and pricked up their ears at every noise from the courtyard.

'They don't like him,' Samson said, his voice low as if

the prisoner might be able to hear him from his cell. 'The sooner he's shipped off to Newgate the better.'

'When will that be?' Titus asked.

'How should I know?'

'Only I was just wonderin' if I might be allowed to sleep in the stables. To . . . er . . . make sure the horses are ready whenever they're required.'

'Well, of course you're sleepin' in the bloody stable. Where else did you think you was? You can go home on a Friday but you must be back at dawn on Monday.'

'Great!'

Titus beamed and Samson glared at him suspiciously.

'Now,' he went over to the door, 'I'm going home to my poor wife. The other lad used to bed down over there.' He pointed to a pallet and straw mattress in the corner. 'You got a blanket?'

Titus shook his head.

'I'll get you a couple from the cells. If it gets too cold go into the kitchen: the door's always open.'

He took the lantern and crossed the courtyard, his heavy boots rapping against the cobbles.

'Who's that trip-trapping across my bridge?' cackled a voice from cell three and Beatrice whinnied in the darkness.

Titus sat down on the mattress. At the bottom of the bed, where the horses could not get at them, were sacks of feed. One of them contained hazelnuts. He'd eaten nothing for two days now. Shuffling to the end of the bed he scooped out a handful of nuts and began pressing them into his mouth.

To his intense embarrassment Samson came back while

he was bending over the sack. He didn't say a word as Titus gulped down the last mouthful, the corners of the nuts scraping down his dry throat.

'Right . . . well . . . here you go.'

The policeman laid a pile of blankets at the end of the mattress and hung a lantern from a nail on the wall. 'If you don't know what you're doing ask one of the stable boys at the Rose and Crown. I don't want the horses lamed by your ignorance.'

'Yes, sir.'

'Well, goodnight, lad,' the older man said, more gently. 'And try and keep warm.'

'Goodnight.'

He went out, closing the lower half of the door behind him. This time his footsteps were quieter and he entered the station via the kitchen instead of walking past the cells.

Titus sat down on the mattress and looked around his new home. It could have been a lot worse. In fact, in many ways it was better than the house in Old Pye Street. It smelled sweeter, the horses were warm and companionable, the walls were clean and dry. So dry, in fact, that the mortar had crumbled entirely from one of the bricks and he was able to slide the whole thing out. The stable boy had clearly used the little cubbyhole as a receptacle for his own treasures for Titus pulled out a dog-eared postcard whose subject matter made him blush. He pushed the postcard to the back of the hole and then took from his pocket the lock of his mother's hair. After tying it in a strand of hay he tucked the hair into the hole and replaced the brick.

Then he dimmed the lantern and lay back on the mattress. It had a comfortable smell of sweat and horses. Suddenly he felt crushingly tired. He mustn't sleep, he told himself, not when Hannah would be wide awake and terrified, thinking he'd abandoned her for good. He forced his eyes to stay open and gazed out through the open half of the door at the moon, a hazy greenish circle through the smog. Perhaps she was looking at it too. His eyelids grew heavier and heavier until it was so much effort to keep them open he decided to rest them by closing them just for a few minutes.

The next thing he knew it was morning.

As soon as he was up and washed he had to prepare the carriage for cell three's prisoner to be transferred to Newgate. A hush descended on the station as the six officers obliged to take the Wigman filed out into the courtyard. But this time there was no struggle. The prisoner walked calmly out of his cell into the semicircle of armed men and allowed himself to be handcuffed.

'Ahhh, what a beautiful morning,' he said, inhaling deeply. 'Now,' he smiled at each one in turn, 'which one of you had honey on his toast this morning?'

Not one of the men would catch the eye that passed over them, except Samson who jerked him roughly by the arm towards the cart.

'I do so love honey,' Rancer sang, as he sauntered across the courtyard, 'especially with eggs.'

Titus stood by Leopold, murmuring words of comfort into his ear. Through the wisps of hair that sprang out from the horse's ear he took a look at the prisoner. He was tall and spindly, like a spider reared up on its back legs, and this impression was intensified by the uniform black of his clothing. His shirt must have been torn in the arrest for it flapped open, revealing a bone-white chest sprouting coarse black hairs like insect legs. His face had the same pallor and his eyes were red-rimmed.

Before stepping inside the box he gave Samson a smile. His teeth were long and yellow against the white of his lips.

'Keep my bed warm for me, handsome.'

Samson swore and kicked him up the backside so hard that he tumbled into the cart. Samson slammed the door then wiped his hands on his jacket, as if they might have picked up some contagion.

The horses were back by noon and while Titus was grooming them Samson came outside and informed him gruffly that he should join them for lunch from now on.

'We each of us pays a penny a week for the pies but the men have agreed to put in a farthing each every fortnight so's you can be fed.'

Titus's grip on the grooming brush tightened.

'I don't need charity, sir.'

'Oh pipe down. The pie'll be there. If you don't come and eat it you'll only be pulling it out of the bin later, stone cold and covered in pipe ash.'

Later, when he heard Samson's bellow announcing the arrival of lunch, Titus slunk into the kitchen and nibbled his meal at a shameful distance from the rest of them. After twenty minutes, however, he was sitting at the table choking on a piece of kidney at one of the constables' lewd story about a girl he'd arrested in Clerkenwell who he first thought was a child prostitute but who turned out to be an ancient dwarf.

'She tried to pinch me arse but couldn't reach no higher than the back of me knee!'

They stopped laughing as Pilbury entered but the half-smile on the Inspector's face made Titus wonder if he'd been listening at the door.

'I want to pay a visit to Rancer's mother in Judas Island,' Pilbury announced. 'See if she can't shed some light on a possible motive. I need someone with some knowledge of the area to accompany me.'

The men looked at one another. Titus knew that some of them had been involved in Rancer's arrest and, by the looks of things, had no desire to revisit the killer's lair any time soon. The police rarely ventured far into Devil's Acre. If they hadn't caught their quarry in the first few streets they generally gave him up as a lost cause.

'I'll come,' Titus said.

All eyes turned to him, mouths stopped chewing.

'Shame on you, boys!' Samson roared at the other men. 'Cowards, the lot of you!'

Some of the men protested and made to get up but Pilbury stopped them.

'Titus will do nicely. He knows the Acre better than any of us. Come on, lad.'

He led Pilbury through the streets of his home patch with a straight spine and a scowl of defiance. Some of the locals scowled back, one or two spat on the ground or muttered a curse, but most melted away at the sight of the policeman's dark coat. After nightfall they would have been braver, and more dangerous. Titus and Hannah would have to be careful when they finally came back. Of all the risky professions practised by the Acre's inhabitants, copper's nark was the most deadly.

They had to pass close to Old Pye Street and, turning into one of the alleys that ran behind it, Titus came face to face with Stitcher. For a moment the two boys simply stared at one another, then Stitcher looked past Titus to Pilbury. His face hardened and he took a step into the centre of the path. Titus felt Pilbury stiffen behind him and he turned back to the policeman:

'Wait, I know him.'

He walked forward, but stopped a few feet from Stitcher, held back by the look on the other boy's face.

'Selling your old friends already, eh?' Stitcher said quietly.

'No. It's not like that.'

'Bollocks.'

Stitcher's hand flickered and then there was a knife in it. Titus moved quickly to block it from the view of the policeman.

'Don't. It's not you he's after. He's here about the murders of those kids.'

For a moment Stitcher did not move, and then, almost imperceptibly, the knife vanished back up his sleeve. His expression remained steely but finally he nodded.

'I'll make sure it's known.'

And then he was gone.

'He looked like a bad lot,' Pilbury said, coming up to join him.

'He's a friend,' Titus said quietly.

The streets grew narrower until the roofs of the buildings cut out all daylight. Brown water seeped from crevices and the patched windows were draped in cobwebs. Occasionally some wretched bundle of sticks and rags would press itself into a doorway to let them pass. There was little fight left in the denizens of this particular part of the Acre. Those who ended up here only left again in a box.

Just when it seemed as if the buildings would crush them, the alley opened out onto a large square. Though Titus had known the way to Judas Island for as long as he could remember, he had rarely visited the spot. It had a bad reputation amidst his superstitious neighbours.

In the middle of the square was a church, a charred and ruinous hulk surrounded by what might once have been a graveyard but was now a rubbish tip enclosed by a rusting railing.

'That's where they lived,' Pilbury said, 'Rancer and his mother.'

They walked up to the railing. The walls of the church were partially intact on the eastern side, but the west side had crumbled to rubble. The porch still stood and the badly weathered inscription above it read:

CAPPELLA
SANCTE MARIA
ROUNCIVALL

Titus spoke quickly before Pilbury could begin translating:

'Chapel of St Mary Rouncivall.'

'I've heard of this place,' Pilbury said, 'though I thought it was long gone. It was the chapel of an old convent hospital. When Henry the Eighth's men came to burn the place down the nuns barricaded themselves in, so the soldiers simply burned it with them in it. Afterwards they claimed the nuns had been practising witchcraft. It's a mystery why the ruins weren't demolished long since.'

'This is the Devil's Acre, sir,' Titus said. 'The whole place is a ruin.'

'I suppose she must be living somewhere over that side.' Pilbury gestured towards the eastern portion of the building. 'I'll go and see what I can get out of her. You wait here.'

'I'm coming with you.'

Pilbury stared at him.

'I won't say nothing and I'll stay out of sight but Samson would have my guts if he thought I'd let you go in alone.'

Pilbury protested, but Titus was already pushing open the gate, wincing as the rusted iron screamed out their presence, and picking his way across the detritus of the graveyard.

He waited for Pilbury at the entrance to the gloomy porch, but walking through it brought them straight back out into the light again. The whole church was a shell, an empty skull.

'How could anyone live here, sir?' Titus whispered. 'No warmth, no shelter from the elements, no privacy to concoct potions.'

Pilbury looked around him, bewildered.

'The men arrested him in the graveyard and it was such a struggle they weren't able to search the place. There must be a roofed section somewhere. Keep looking.'

They spread out, Pilbury moving further into what must have been the nave of the chapel while Titus skirted around the eastern wall, stepping over flagstones pushed vertical by tree roots until they resembled huge teeth.

'She must have gone already,' Pilbury called after a few minutes. 'We're wasting our time.'

Titus began picking his way back to the porch. Forced to take a detour past an explosion of brambles his ankle suddenly sheared and he was pitched onto his backside. He looked around for a rat hole or tree root, but found, to his surprise, that he had stumbled on the first step of a staircase leading down into darkness.

No, not quite darkness.

Deep down in the abyss a greyish light wavered and the damp air rising up from below stank of tallow.

'Mr Pilbury,' he called softly, 'I think she lives in the crypt.'

Pilbury came over to join him and they both peered down into the depths. Darkness flowed up to meet them like smoke.

'Come on, then, but keep your wits about you.'

Their feet on the steps were like the cracks of a rifle. Titus wasn't superstitious but all the way down he had the very strong sensation of being watched. When they got to the bottom of the staircase a long brick corridor stretched ahead of them.

All was silent. There was not even the ticking of a beetle or the scurry of mice as they passed down the corridor towards the wavering grey light at the end. As his eyes became accustomed to the gloom Titus noticed that the walls were not bare. Beside him was a plaster death mask of some crone, the eyes sewn shut, the toothless mouth grinning. Further on was a large bone, black with age and carved with some intricate language he could not read. What looked like a human foetus grown almost to full term turned out to be the desiccated corpse of a monkey, nailed up by its little brown hands. Its eyes, which must have dried out and fallen into its skull, had been replaced by pieces of mirror.

He pressed himself against the opposite wall to pass it, only to brush against a clutch of chicken feathers, their tips caked with dried blood. He couldn't stop a gasp of horror escaping his lips as he jerked away.

'Don't be afraid,' Pilbury murmured. 'This mumbo-jumbo has no power to hurt you.'

'I know,' Titus said, trying to keep his voice steady.

The smell of pig fat grew stronger and now he could make out the back wall of the tunnel some way ahead. Frail yellow light fell from an opening just to the right of it. He began to hear, over the pounding of his heart, a rhythmic clicking, like that of a beetle or cockroach. He tried to swallow the panic that rose up at the thought of them scuttling around his feet.

The Inspector's pace slowed as they approached the end of the tunnel, his black silhouette a reassuring barrier between Titus and whatever lay beyond. Only the tips of his boots gleamed, unblemished amidst the filth.

He stopped just short of the rectangle of light that fell on the floor and murmured, 'Stay here. Use your eyes and your ears.'

Then he stepped into the light.

Titus pressed himself against the wall and eased along it until he had a view of the room beyond.

The old woman sat on a wooden chair in the middle of the room, knitting with invisible thread. A fire burning low on the floor in front of her cast the only light. Lining the walls were shelves that stretched off into the darkness. The shelves were filled with lumpen shapes: a jawbone, a pelvis, a skull.

The ceiling was low enough that Pilbury had to hunch his shoulders. Rancer must have scuttled around the place on all fours.

'What are you knitting, madam?' Pilbury said.

'The hair of children. If a barren woman secretes such a patch inside her girdle she shall become fertile.'

There was something strange about the way she spoke, as if she was trying to swallow something large or unpalatable, and now, as she squinted up at the policeman, Titus could see that the knot of her shawl was forcing her head over to one side.

The smell of honey was strong and he noticed, beside her stool, a large glass jar filled with an amber substance. Floating in this viscous liquid was the body of a cat. Goosebumps rose up on his arms.

'Is that honey, madam?' Pilbury said, his voice light.

'Honey is a natural preserver, of body and spirit. The ancient Egyptians could revive a person who had been so embalmed, even after many years had passed,' she said. Then added quickly, 'This wisdom is lost to us now, of course.'

'But clearly you believe,' Pilbury said, gesturing to the cat.

'That is Osiris,' the woman croaked, following his gaze. 'The best and most loved of my darlings.'

As she turned her head Titus could see that the knot at her throat was not the fabric of her shawl but an enormous excrescence of flesh, criss-crossed with swollen veins. He recoiled from the sight and her eyes darted, quick as fleas, in his direction.

He drew back and waited a moment or two before peeping round the wall again. She was smiling at him. His scalp crawled.

The Inspector seemed unperturbed.

'Where did you get the hair?' he asked. 'From your son?'

'His hair is black, Officer Pilbury.'

'Did he give it to you after he had torn it from the heads of the children he murdered?'

She did not pause in her knitting. The rasp of the needles was like the sharpening of knives.

'I bought this from a little one who wanted the money for a dolly.'

'What was her name?'

'Esther. Esther Herring.'

Pilbury took a notebook from his pocket and wrote in it. As he wrote, almost offhandedly he said, 'Your son will be hanged, madam. Is there anything you can tell me that might mitigate the severity of his punishment?'

'The poor lamb did not know what he was doing,' she crooned.

'So you think he was coerced? That he was the instrument of another?'

'Oh no, no. I mean he is as simple as the blossom on the trees and would not know the error of his ways. Surely in these modern times we do not destroy those whose only weakness is their own poor mind?'

She leaned down and picked up a tumbler of water. It might have been the thickness of the cheap glass but the water inside looked an unhealthy shade of green. She sipped it then placed it back down without taking her eyes off Pilbury.

'Your son is perfectly sane, Mrs Rancer. Whilst in my care he has displayed reason and cunning. Last week he pretended sickness then wounded one of my officers with a spoon he had secreted from his meal and filed to a point on the wall.'

'It is not of my doing, sir. His father was a brute who knocked the sense out of the poor lad before he was weaned.'

'If this is so, then the father must be punished. Where is he now?'

'Dead.'

The needles click-clacked and the woman's breath laboured on its passage through her misshapen throat. Titus became aware of scratching behind him and he almost cried out in terror. Turning around he saw two bright eyes low on the ground about three feet away from him. He kicked out but the eyes did not blink. He shrank back against the wall as the scratching resumed and the thing came closer. Surely the claws that made that noise were too large for a rat. When it came far enough into the dim sphere of light he almost laughed out loud. A chicken. The stringy bird went past him into the room and strutted fearlessly into the blackness beyond the firelight.

'Tell me why he did it,' Pilbury went on. 'For the sake of those children's loved ones.'

Mrs Rancer laughed, a guttural wheeze that made the hairs on Titus's back rise up and press against his sweat-cold shirt.

'They had no loved ones. They were nothing but flotsam.'

Pilbury stared at her.

'You are a wicked woman.'

The needles stopped. The air suddenly congealed until it was too thick to breathe. Titus felt a brown claw close around his heart.

'As you are not of a mind to assist me,' Pilbury said evenly, 'I will, for now at least, bid you goodnight.'

A minute later they were out in the almost-fresh air again.

'Honey,' Pilbury said as they picked their way back to the porch, almost to himself. 'The rags he stuffed down their throats were soaked in honey. A preserver of life . . .'

They passed through the porch and into the graveyard.

'But no eggs,' he went on.

Titus stared at him but Pilbury did not seem inclined to elaborate on the strange comment.

'There was a chicken,' Titus said.

Pilbury stopped walking.

'It came past me when you were talking to the old woman. At first I thought it was a monster!'

He laughed at his own foolishness, and with it came a wonderful release of tension.

'A demon perhaps,' Pilbury said thoughtfully. 'Chickens are traditional familiars for witches.'

As they stepped through the gate and out into the silent square Titus prayed that he would never have to go down into that hole again as long as he lived.

# 9

# YELLOW JACKETS

Though it seemed to take years, Friday afternoon finally arrived. Titus burst out of the gate at five and hurtled along Victoria Street.

At least the porter would not recognise him. His clothes were even cleaner than when his mother had bought them from the ragman, thanks to the pungent green hand soap in the station bathroom, and his hair was unrecognisably sleek and springy. He had put on weight and working in the sun of the courtyard had taken away some of his pallor. He strode past the file of miserable applicants and straight into the porter's anteroom.

'Afternoon, sir,' he said briskly. 'I should like to see Hannah Adams.'

The porter did not look up from his ledger.

'Visiting hours is nine till noon.'

'I'm sorry, I was unaware of this. Perhaps you could make an exception. I've come a long way.'

The man looked up at him wearily.

'Older brother, are you?'

Good. He did not recognise him.

'Yes.'

'Then I will make an exception, but not for the sake of

your legs, boy. Adams is already on reduced rations. If her behaviour does not improve she will placed in solitary confinement. If you have any influence on her at all I would advise you to exert it now.' He sighed and went back to the ledger. 'We do not enjoy inflicting pain on one so young.'

Titus could utter no reply and waited dumbly while the man rang a bell and the young nurse he had seen that first night appeared.

'He's here to see Adams,' the porter said.

The nurse led Titus through endless dingy corridors. His eyes had just grown accustomed to the gloom when they reached a door and a moment later burst out into the daylight. The yard was divided into two portions, with the men and boys occupying the left side and the women and girls on the right.

'Wait here. I'll get her.'

She walked away from him towards a sea of white caps. The girls' uniforms, of striped aprons with dark skirts and blouses and great black boots, made them indistinguishable from one another, except in height.

Gathered in a small group around an elderly nurse were the infants, all dressed in the regulation uniform, right down to the baby in striped swaddling. Some listened to the story she was reading, others drew with chalk on the ground, two fought over a wretched doll made from a lump of wood.

Off to the left of them were the slightly bigger girls. Too old to escape work they were all sewing, their heads bent, in silence. He watched them for a while, searching for Hannah, but in all that time none of them exchanged a titter or a murmur.

A sharp male voice made him turn his head. In the far corner of the yard was a long table, behind which sat a line of young women unravelling lengths of tarry rope into dirty strands that could be reused. One of the male officers was reprimanding a girl for her idleness. She had folded her arms and was staring at him with a look of such insolence that eventually he struck her face with the crop he was holding. Her head snapped back but a moment later she had composed herself, refolding her arms and fixing him with the same look of contempt, even as blood trickled down into her left eye. He gave up and walked briskly away. A burly, hard-faced nurse was stationed at either end of the table: presumably these were the troublesome ones. Some wore the yellow jackets that marked them out as prostitutes or women who had birthed out of wedlock: a few of these were as young as Hannah. One was entirely obscured by the ball of oakum before her and he could just see her thin white fingers tugging at the strands. His heart jumped into his mouth.

Sure enough the young nurse picked her way behind the table, eventually stopping by the hidden figure, bending and speaking to her. The fingers froze for a moment then resumed their work. The nurse came back over to him and said with some satisfaction, 'She will not see you.'

'Hannah!' he called across the yard. The fingers did not pause.

'Go and fetch her,' he said to the nurse.

'I'm not at your beck and call.'

'Then . . . then tell her I will come back tomorrow and she'd better be ready to speak to me or . . . or . . . or there'll be trouble for her.'

The nurse smirked.

'Gloria's thrashed her twice already this week,' she nodded at one of the burly women at the end of the table, 'and she didn't utter a peep. A skinny little streak like you is hardly gonna have her quaking in her boots.'

It took Titus a while to swallow his anger and shame and the burning desire to run at that great ugly bully of a woman and beat his fists into her fat belly. Eventually he had composed himself enough to speak.

'Then please tell her there will be a currant bun waiting for her.'

The nurse sniffed and stared at him.

'And for yourself, of course.'

Back in the porter's room he almost told the man he would take Hannah there and then. Perhaps he could sneak her into the stables with him and feed her with his own lunch and the scraps left by the other men. But it couldn't work. Samson was in and out of the stables and, besides, Titus would be so busy worrying about what she was up to he'd never be able to concentrate on the job. If he ended up getting himself dismissed then where would they be?

He slunk out of the office and through the bleak court-yard feeling as low as he'd done when they first arrived.

That night he slept fitfully, keeping half an ear out for the chimes of Big Ben. As soon as they struck six he was up and seeing to the horses. If he completed his chores by half past eight he could nip out to see Hannah and be back by the time the men had finished their breakfast.

But it soon became apparent he was going nowhere today. By eight the station was swarming with activity. The jury in the Rancer trial had retired the previous night and the verdict was due to be delivered in a few hours.

The atmosphere at the station was buoyant as the men frantically completed their tasks so as to be allowed to accompany the Inspector to court. The general feeling was that he was certain to be found guilty and sent to the gallows, and so the men had recovered their boldness a little.

Titus was ordered here and there to pass messages or fetch ink or boot polish, and barely had time to prepare Beatrice and Leopold for the journey.

By one o'clock the entire station was deserted as the men bundled onto the carriage that would take them to court. The yard echoed with laughter and banter, as if they were off to see a man married rather than condemned. Only Pilbury's face was grim as he emerged into the grey afternoon.

'Are you worried he'll get off?' Titus asked him as the Inspector came around to pat the horses.

'Oh, they'll convict him and hang him.'

'That's good, isn't it?'

'Just another death, boy,' Pilbury sighed as he put on his top hat. 'There are so many.'

He climbed up onto the carriage and Titus opened the gate for them.

As it clanged shut Big Ben struck half past the hour. He was too late to see Hannah. He trudged back to the deserted stables and curled up on his bed with his face to the wall.

# 10

# A VISITOR

The week passed agonisingly slowly. The cart was called out barely a handful of times as most of the prisoners, drunks and wife beaters and pickpockets were brought in by the beat officers. At breakfast on Wednesday morning Pilbury came into the station kitchen.

'I'll be leaving for Newgate shortly, if anyone wants to accompany me.'

There was a pause in the muffled crunching of toast, then a general shrugging of shoulders and mumbled excuses. Titus could feel the Inspector's eyes pass over him and he concentrated all his attention on wiping a blob of strawberry jam from his cuff.

'Cowards,' Pilbury said with a smirk and went out.

After the Inspector had gone Samson sent Titus to the market for more hay for the horses, but he hadn't got further than the end of the street when he came face to face with Stitcher, piggybacking Charly. When he saw Titus, Charly scrambled off Stitcher's back then ran straight up and kicked him in the shins.

The two older boys regarded one another in silence. Eventually Stitcher broke it.

'So, you was there for the Wigman, then.'

'I told you, didn't I?'

'And now you're workin' for the police.'

His black eyes bored into Titus but his voice was expressionless.

'Yes.'

He eased onto his back foot, ready to run. There was no sense fighting Stitcher who was stronger, quicker and always carried a knife.

'It's OK,' Stitcher said.

Titus blinked.

'I knew you'd never stay with us,' Stitcher went on and Titus could tell by the pulled down corners of his mouth that it cost him a lot to say it.

'If it were just me, Stitch . . .'

'I know.'

'And I swear on Ma's grave that I will never, ever . . .'

'I know.'

For a while after that Stitcher seemed very interested in a piece of lichen that was peeling off the wall.

'So, er, what you doin'?'

Stitcher perked up immediately.

'Goin' to the hangin'. Aren't you? I'd've thought you lot'd get pride of place up the front!'

'I wouldn't want it.'

Stitcher blinked at him. 'Why?'

Titus shrugged. 'I've seen enough of him to last a lifetime.'

Stitcher's mouth spread into a leer.

'Scared of him, were ya?'

'No!'

'Scaredy-cat, scaredy-cat!' Charly chanted.

'I wasn't scared,' Titus sighed, trying to sound weary instead of defensive.

'Well, if you ain't scared come along with us and watch the bugger dance.'

Stitcher smiled but the smile was faltering and when he spoke again his voice had lost its jeering edge. 'For old times' sake.'

Titus glanced back at the station. Even from here he could hear Samson bawling out one of the junior officers. Well, he thought, swallowing hard, Samson would just have to lump it.

'Come on, then.'

It was too far to walk so they jumped on an omnibus heading towards the city. When the conductor came for their fares Stitcher stared pointedly at Titus and he rooted around in his pocket for the money Samson had given him for the hay. Then they climbed the narrow stairs to the cheap seats on top.

It was cold up there, and the damp air soon saturated their clothes. Charly climbed onto Stitcher's lap and Stitcher pulled his jacket around the smaller boy's narrow shoulders. As they drew near the river a thick fog rolled in, concealing the road and the lower part of the coach from sight and deadening all sound, until Titus felt as if he was being rowed across a silent sea. The muffled rumble of the wheels on the muddy road was like the hiss of oars through still water. He shivered and pulled his jacket tight across his chest.

'So, the Rancers, eh?' he said, to break the silence.

Stitcher gave a low whistle. 'Rosie says she reckons he might have had his brain addled by all the knocks his dad give him.'

'Dead isn't he, the dad?'

Stitcher nodded. 'Rosie says the witch murdered him. Well, that's what he told everyone down the Archer anyway.'

'Who did?'

'Rancer Senior told his mates at the pub that his wife was murdering him with a curse but he was too scared to do anything about it, and a week later he up and died.'

'Not much of a bully, then?'

'Only to the boy. He was scared of the wife so he took it out on the boy. Terrible things. Joseph started off at the school where you went, but he got so many knocks about the head by his pa that in the end he couldn't remember which way up was Tuesday, so he stopped going and went to help his ma instead. Used to collect the stuff for her spells. The odd chicken bone here or a bit of hair. Rancer Senior didn't like it. Two against one, he said. So he decided to scare the boy out of his wits and put him off witchcraft once and for all. He was a gravedigger up at St Bride's, so one night he took the boy up to a grave what he'd just dug. A his-and-hers plot, you know? And the wife had been buried years before. Well, Rancer Senior took the boy and threw him in the hole next to the old coffin. Rotten it was and you could see the skellington through the planks. It was raining cats and dogs, and every time the boy tried to get out he slipped down into the mud. The next morning they found him floating in a foot of water with the corpse's arms around his neck. They thought he was dead from the shock. Took all his mother's potions and mumbo-jumbo to bring him back. She never forgave the old man. She would have made him suffer longer if she could, but

– according to Rosie – one day she found him beating the boy with an iron poker, so she finished him there and then. One word and his heart stopped. Course it was a heart attack so the police couldn't do nothing. But the whole Acre knew it was her. And she wanted them to.'

He gave a little shudder and his arms tightened around Charly, who was falling asleep.

'It's a bad time all round,' he went on, lowering his voice. 'Did you hear about Ronnie?'

'No.'

'Only got word of it a few days ago, though it happened a while back I think. He were down in the hold of one of the ships he was building when half the deck came down on his head. They only recognised him from that tattoo on his back . . . You know? The one with the Sea Monster. Titus . . .? You all right?'

Titus swallowed a few times to wet his suddenly dry throat. Had Ronnie been dead by the time of the medium's show at the Palace?

'Yeh. I'm fine.'

'There's St Paul's,' Stitcher said. 'We'd better get down.'

He picked up the dozing Charly and they went down the stairs, stepping off into the swirling fog. Up here, away from the river and the factories of the south bank, the smell wasn't so choking; just coal and woodsmoke and the faint perfume of incense. Titus followed Stitcher along the unfamiliar streets until their progress was stopped by a large crowd. The hubbub woke Charly, who wiped his nose on his brother's lapel and hopped down.

'What's going on?' Stitcher asked a tall man craning his neck to see over the heads of those in front of him.

'They ain't opened the gates yet but you can hear him singing when it goes quiet.'

Titus shrank back. Perhaps he could lose the other two in the crowd and slope back to the police station before he had to hear any more of that awful crooning, but then there was a sudden commotion from the front and the crowd surged forward.

'They've opened the gates!' cried the man, and lunged towards the press of backs, entirely oblivious to the fact that Charly had just pinched his pocket watch.

'This way!' Stitcher cried and led them around the edge of the mass of people to cut in near the front, at which point he began crying out that he'd lost his sister.

'Mary-Ann!' he hollered. 'Where are you, littl'un? Oh Christ, she's only three! MARY-ANN!'

Concerned onlookers opened up a path that led directly through to the front of the yard. Titus's footsteps hesitated when he saw the looming scaffold. Two thick black posts rose up from it, and dangling from the crossbeam between them was a single noose, swaying gently in the breeze.

As the crowd began to pack in around them silence fell, as if an invisible blanket had settled upon them, muting all sound. Feet shuffled. Someone coughed. Charly pushed himself between the older boys and slipped his hands into theirs. His hands felt very cold and small. He was staring up at the scaffold, blinking quickly with those wide blue eyes. The chain of the pocket watch dangled, forgotten, from his pocket.

'Will he fall on us?' he said to Stitcher.

'Don't be stupid,' Stitcher said, but gave his hand a squeeze.

Fog crept between them, curling its pale fingers into Charly's hair and winding around Stitcher's throat. With it came a thin, cold wind that made the noose swing jauntily. A movement from above caught Titus's eye and he saw that the walls of the prison were bristling with crows, their black eyes glittering as they glared down at the scaffold. Then, as one, their slick, black heads turned.

'Can we go home, Stitch?' Charly said. 'I don't like it.'

With a sigh of irritation Stitcher picked him up and the smaller boy hid his face in his brother's neck.

Then the high, clear voice of a child singing cut through the silence.

'Jesus' love never failed me yet, never failed me yet . . .'

A priest was walking slowly from the entrance to the gaol towards the scaffold. Had he brought a choirboy with him, Titus wondered; how strange. But then the priest's steps turned and goosebumps prickled down Titus's back. Behind the priest, walking between him and the executioner, was a spindly figure.

'There's one thing I know,' the piping voice continued, from Rancer's black mouth, 'for he loves me so . . .'

All Rancer's hair had been shaved off, leaving areas of black stubble, like patches of rot on a piece of fruit.

The singing subsided into childish giggles which deepened until they became the ugly rasping cackle that had so chilled the atmosphere of the station.

The priest began climbing the scaffold and the wood groaned beneath him. Rancer went next, his footsteps utterly silent as if he were gliding over the wood. He had been bound so tightly that the hands tied at his back had turned blue. Finally came the hangman, short and squat as a tree stump, his expression completely blank. He positioned Rancer behind the noose and busied himself checking the various parts of the structure. Rancer stood motionless, facing out towards the crowd. For a moment there was such a deep silence that everyone in the yard must have heard his next words.

'So many come to watch my little dance,' he chuckled. 'At least three of you should learn the steps since it will be your turn soon enough.'

Stitcher leaned across to Titus and breathed, 'Reckon he's talking about me and Charly?' He grinned but Charly whimpered and clung on tighter.

Titus tried to respond but his throat had gone bone dry. Almost imperceptibly the crowd edged backwards and moved closer to one another.

Somewhere in the distance a bell began to toll mournfully, and seemed to take an eternity to strike its nine beats.

As Rancer's gaze scoured the yard Titus was paralysed with terror lest he should be recognised, but the killer's eye was caught elsewhere. A group of top-hatted men stood slightly apart from the rest of the crowd, in a roped-off area beside the scaffold. Titus's heart jumped as he saw the Inspector. Would Rancer scream abuse at him? Or throw curses until they were choked off by the rope?

But then Rancer did the most astonishing thing.

He smiled. He bowed. He tried to raise a hand but, because of the binding, just managed a twitch of the shoulder. The acrid aroma of his sweat reached those in the front row.

'Be seeing you,' he said to Pilbury.

To his credit the Inspector did not flinch or avert his

gaze and their eyes remained locked until the hangman stepped forward and pulled the bag over Rancer's head. From the prisoner's stance, alert and watchful, Titus couldn't shake the feeling that he was still staring at Pilbury.

This was the part he had been dreading. Would Rancer finally break down, beg for mercy, sob for his mother, wet himself? That was the worst bit about a hanging, the reason why he and Hannah stopped going. You ended up feeling sorry for even the worst specimens of humanity: Hannah had once cried for days over a young mother who had poisoned her children.

But Rancer stood patiently while the hangman did his business, as if he were patiently submitting to some minor inconvenience. He scuffed at some sawdust with his toe while the noose was being looped up, whistled as the rope was placed around his neck, then sauntered over to the hatch as if he were positioning himself for a kiss under the mistletoe. Titus found it impossible to feel any pity for him, only a sort of ghastly awe.

The priest raised his hand and said in a flat voice, 'May God have mercy on your soul.'

There were no last words of comfort and support from the executioner. Not even the customary entreaty to 'be brave'. Without so much as a pat on the back, he kicked the lever that operated the door, Rancer dropped like a stone and the rope snapped taut with a thud.

Titus was dimly aware that, beside him, Charly had begun to cry but he could not tear his gaze from the hooded face.

For several moments afterwards he half expected Rancer's body to give a convulsion and leap onto the platform again, tearing off the rope and hood to leer out at them – *fooled you!* But the neck must have instantly broken because there was not the slightest twitch. The corpse only turned in a slow circle in the cold morning air. Gradually the fingers of fog crawled up the scaffold to envelop it in a shroud of grey and the rest of the grim business of cutting him down was hidden from the crowd.

Titus blinked and took a deep, shuddering breath. It couldn't have taken more than a minute or two from start to finish but his aching body felt as if it had been standing at the same spot for hours.

The crowd began to disperse in silence.

'That were smartly done,' Stitcher said, his voice uncharacteristically low. 'They were lucky his head din't shear clean off. All I can say is that they must have been in a great hurry to get rid of him.'

They wandered back down towards the river but none of them felt much like talking and Charly was still crying. At the corner of the Strand and Newcastle Street, Stitcher asked half-heartedly if he fancied a drink but Titus said he ought to be getting back to the station. Stitcher didn't seem to mind, merely shrugged, hoisted Charly onto the other hip and wandered away in the direction of the Acre. Titus watched them gradually disappear into the fog, then he turned his steps towards Covent Garden to spend what was left of Samson's hay money.

The following day was very quiet, and on Friday morning Titus crossed his fingers and slipped out without asking, his pocket filled with buns he had somewhat shamefacedly asked Inspector Pilbury for. Big Ben struck eight as he arrived at the workhouse gates. They were open and the courtyard was already bustling. This time people were coming out of the porter's door, their faces pink and radiant with the determination that they would not return. Before them lay another full day that, if spent well, might set them back on their feet again. Titus held the door open for the Irishwoman and her children who'd been behind them in the queue the night they arrived and she beamed and blessed him.

Even the porter looked cheerful, waving off his charges with wishes of luck and good health. He greeted Titus politely and soon the nurse arrived to take him through to the yard.

They walked through corridors that smelled of a mixture of over-boiled cabbage and bleach until they reached a door. Here the nurse stopped and stood with her back to it. He reached into his pocket and drew out the smaller of the buns.

'Much obliged,' she said, snatching it with an acid smile.

This time, to Titus's relief, Hannah was sewing with the younger girls. Her head darted up the minute the nurse spoke to her. She quickly rolled the fabric up and tucked it into her apron pocket, before following the nurse across the yard.

'Where's me bun?' she said, as soon as they were alone.

She was thinner and paler and a bruise yellowed her cheek.

'Look, I know you're angry with me,' he said, 'but who do you think I'm doing this for?'

'I don't give a monkey's. Where's me bun?'

Sighing, he took the little yellow bun from his pocket and held it out to her.

'Where's the currants?'

'I could only get saffron.'

'I hate saffron.'

'Very well. I'll take it back, then.'

But before he could withdraw it she snatched it from his hand and set upon it ravenously.

'You'd get more to eat if you behaved,' he said.

She gave him a filthy look but didn't pause in her chewing to reply, so he took the opportunity to speak to her without getting any backchat.

'I got a job. With Inspector Pilbury.'

Her chewing slowed down for a moment.

'It pays thruppence a week. That means I shall soon have the deposit for the room. And as soon as I do I'll come and get you and we'll be together again.'

Her response was muffled by the bun but there was no mistaking the sarcasm: 'Oh good.'

'And who knows, maybe Pilbury will like me enough to make me a constable one day. Then we'd be laughing.'

'Ha,' Hannah said drily, swallowing the last mouthful of bun. 'Got any more?'

'No, but I'll bring you a pie next time. If you can manage to be a bit more civil.'

She sighed heavily.

'Is that a yes?'

She gave a tight little nod.

'Good. Right, well, I'd better get back.'

Hannah took something out of her pocket and slipped it into his.

'What's that, a present?'

'Yeah, course, a present for my loving brother.'

He took it out and began to open it.

'No!' She stayed his hand. 'I don't want to see it. Open it somewhere else.'

He put it away and, before she could stop him, bent and kissed her quickly on the cheek.

'Goodbye, Hannah.'

He smiled as she stomped away scouring her cheek with her sleeve.

Back in the station, Titus made straight for the bathroom where he scrubbed his hands and face until the workhouse stink was no longer in his nostrils. As he washed, he could hear a man remonstrating with the duty officer.

'Every minute she's here she's missing out on earnings somewhere else,' the voice snapped. It was somehow familiar.

'Well, I'm sure Mr Pilbury will not keep her longer than he needs to.'

'He'd better not or—'

The duty officer interrupted him. 'Sit down, sir, or I will ask you to leave.'

Heading back down the passage towards the stables, Titus heard voices coming from Inspector Pilbury's office. It was not unusual for the Inspector to work late, but none of the other officers stayed unless it was their shift, and in that case they would be out on their beats. Some new and important case, perhaps? He paused at the door.

'Are you sure there's nothing I can get you to make you more comfortable? A blanket? It is a chilly night.'

'I won't feel the cold.'

It was a girl's voice, low and melodic. Pilbury was not

speaking to her as a suspect, nor in the businesslike tone he reserved for witnesses. Titus crouched and peered through the keyhole. The room was much darker than usual, and a single small lantern set beneath the table threw so many unexpected shadows on the walls it took him a few moments to realise there were only two people seated inside. Pilbury was not in his usual spot behind the desk, but sitting on the other side of it, his knees almost touching those of a girl. Her skin was pale as milk, her hair coal black. It took Titus a while to recognise her but when she cast an anxious glance at the door he was certain.

'We won't be disturbed, will we?' she said.

'Absolutely not. My men have only just set out on their beats and the front door is locked.'

'I'm ready, then. Do you have the clothing?'

'Yes. I'm sorry it is so dirty, but after a week in the water . . .'

The medium took the grubby rag he held out to her: a threadbare little vest with a butterfly embroidered on the breast, green now, like the rest of the garment. She passed it back and forth through her hands then pressed it to her face and inhaled deeply. Then she flashed one last glance at the door. Titus was momentarily pinned to the spot by eyes so deep and clear you might fall through them and never reach the bottom. He was sure she had seen his own wide eye blinking back but then she turned to the Inspector, placed the vest in her lap and bowed her head.

'Wait till you hear my breathing change.'

For some minutes nothing happened. The medium's breathing continued slow and even, until Titus wondered if she had fallen asleep. Pilbury, on the other hand, was alert as a cat. His breath came in snatches and, in the light of the small lantern, Titus could see sweat beading his forehead.

And then the most peculiar smell filled the room, casting its tendrils through the keyhole to make Titus gag. It was the smell of soot and fish and tallow and rotting vegetables and blood and excrement and all the other myriad smells of the city combined in a briny soup. It was the smell of the Thames.

Someone gasped. Titus's eye darted around his tiny sphere of vision to discover this third person he had not noticed before, but there was no sign of anyone. The shadows had become remarkably still.

And then a voice, a child's voice, let out a long, agonised sob.

Titus's blood slowed to a crawl as he watched the girl's mouth close at the very same moment that terrible cry petered out. Her eyes were wide, straining in their sockets as they skittered around the room. For a second or two Titus's heart actually felt like it had stopped as he waited for them to fall on him, but there was too much panic in them to settle on anything.

'It's all right, little one,' Pilbury said gently. 'My name is William, and I am a policeman. You are safe with me.'

Now the child was weeping.

'Did somebody try to hurt you, sweetheart?'

The girl froze.

'Mamma!'

The chilling howl of despair sent Titus scrabbling back from the keyhole.

'It's all right,' Pilbury said.

Returning to the keyhole Titus saw the Inspector lean forward as if to touch the medium, but then stay his hand.

'Listen to me, child,' Pilbury began again, firmer this time. 'If you wish me to find your mama you must tell me your name.'

The child continued weeping.

'What is your name, girl?'

The child – the medium – flinched.

'Come now, answer me. What is your name?'

The medium unbent her head. Her features were stretched into a mask of terror. Even from here Titus could see the halo of white around her irises – they seemed to have lightened, were now more blue than brown. Her lips opened as wide as the jaw would allow and the scream that ripped out of her mouth made Titus grip the brass door handle.

Pilbury recovered himself after a moment and tried to speak, but his words were drowned in the torrent of noise.

Somewhere beneath it Titus could hear the stable doors shuddering, as if the horses were throwing themselves against them. His brain thrummed and pressed against his skull. Soon his eardrums would surely burst.

And then, as quickly as it had begun, the scream ceased. Pilbury slumped back in his chair. Titus rested his forehead against the cool wood of the door.

The medium rolled back her shoulders and rubbed the corner of her jaw as if it ached a little.

'Did you get what you needed?'

Her voice was her own once more.

'No. She was too distressed.'

'I'm sorry. Would you like me to try again?'

'No.'

'Perhaps someone will come and identify her soon. Don't be upset by what you heard, Mr Pilbury. Remember she's only recently passed over and in a most traumatic manner, and there are many good and kind souls with her now who will soothe her and—'

She suddenly broke off and made a choking sound.

'Miss Kent?'

She did not reply. And then her spine suddenly went rigid. A moment later her head jerked back as if it had been forced.

'Miss Kent! What is it?'

The tendons on her neck bulged and her eyes rolled back into her head. A heaving sound came from the pit of her stomach, echoing around the silent room. Pilbury stared at the medium in horror as she began making the most dreadful choking sounds.

The Inspector did not seem to know what to do. He went to touch her, then pulled back and just repeated her name, imploring her to wake up. Now her throat was bulging, pressing the blue veins to the surface of her skin until Titus could see them pulsing rapidly. Suddenly she gave a last groan, so deep and guttural it was almost a snarl, and something emerged from her mouth.

For a moment nothing moved. The air that trickled through the keyhole to Titus had turned icy cold, the girl was still and silent as a corpse.

Then Pilbury let out a cry of excitement.

'Ah! Is it you again, my poor little soul? Have you come to tell me who you are?'

It was the same thing Titus had witnessed at the theatre.

A strip of white fabric; flattish and long enough to coil around itself, like the dressing for a wound or a winding sheet. It moved sinuously, dancing in front of the Inspector, then reared its head and made a jab at Pilbury's face.

'Ah!' the Inspector pulled away. 'Now that you are free of our mortal coil you are feeling playful. How I understand!'

The river stench had vanished and the smell that now pervaded the Inspector's office, creeping through the keyhole into Titus's own nostrils, was altogether sweeter.

More and more of the stuff emerged from the girl's throat, coiling around her waist like a winding sheet, then peeping almost coyly over her shoulder, making Pilbury chuckle.

If Pilbury wasn't afraid then perhaps there was no reason to be, thought Titus. He let out his breath. The serpent went suddenly still. Then it turned its splayed head towards the door and slid noiselessly over the girl's shoulder into her lap. There it hesitated for a moment over the still white hands and, if it had eyes, they would have been fixed on the keyhole. Pilbury was still watching its every move, a bewitched smile playing about his lips. The hairs on Titus's neck rose and very slowly he moved away from the aperture.

He only heard what happened next.

'Is this really the girl from the river, or are you a different spirit?' Pilbury continued in a low voice that suddenly became harsher. 'Do not play games with me. Swaying your head like a cobra will not scare me. You are wasting valuable time that could be spent discovering the identity of one of Rancer's—'

But he did not finish. There was a quiet *shoosh*, like a stone flying by your ear, and then the policeman gave a strangled cry and retched violently. Chair legs screamed over the floorboards and there were muffled thumps and knocks as if two large men were fighting. All the while the ghastly retching went on and on.

Then it stopped.

Titus leaped to his feet and kicked the door open. The medium was slumped senseless on the chair. Pilbury lay on the floor at her feet, his face white. There was no-one else in the room and the serpent thing had vanished.

'Sir?'

He flung himself down and grasped the Inspector's hand. It was ice-cold.

'Can you hear me?'

A bubble of bloody spittle appeared in the corner of the policeman's mouth. At least that meant he was still breathing.

Titus vaulted the desk and began rifling through the drawers and cupboards for smelling salts or snuff or brandy. In his haste papers fluttered across the room and ink pots spilled on the floor.

And then, without warning, Pilbury jerked awake with a cry, as if he had just awoken from a nightmare.

He swallowed, grimaced, then blinked once or twice.

'Sir? Inspector? Are you all right?'

'Of course I'm all right. What the hell are you doing, boy?'

The policeman sprang to his feet without the slightest wobble.

'You seemed . . . unwell. I was looking for smelling salts.'

Then the medium gave a faint moan.

'Me? Look to the girl! She is in need of immediate medical attention. Run to Doctor Hadsley at once!'

By the time Titus returned with the doctor the medium was awake and sipping milky tea that smelled of whisky. With her was the manager he'd seen at the Palace who, Titus now realised, had been the man complaining to the duty officer.

'This is exactly what I warned you about,' he barked in the girl's face. 'Now you ain't got the energy to visit Lady Berkley's so that's fifteen bob down the swanny.'

In his anger the upper-crust accent had entirely disappeared.

Doctor Hadsley was disapproving in his diagnosis that she would be wise to restrict her spiritual wanderings to Sunday mass. Pilbury told the doctor to restrict his opinions to those concerning the body and to leave the soul to those who knew better. The doctor replied that a police officer should be a man of science not superstition. Titus busied himself tidying the papers and doing his best to clean up the ink that had already stained the floorboards.

Eventually the doctor departed, shaking his head.

'Right, come on then,' the girl's manager snapped, gripping her arm and pulling her towards the office door. But at the threshold she wriggled free of him and turned back to Pilbury.

'Are you sure you saw nothing untoward?'

'Nothing at all,' Pilbury said.

She nodded, hesitated a moment, then turned to go.

Titus was sent after them to unlock the gate and hail

them a cab. He was surprised to hear the man give the driver an address in Fulham. The Inspector must value her very highly to bother with the time and expense of getting her here. After all, mediums were two-a-penny nowadays.

As he helped her into the carriage she hesitated, searching his face. Titus smiled politely and she smiled back, frowning a little as if trying to place him. There was a little more colour to her cheeks now and her hand was warm in his own. She stepped inside and he shut the door.

Returning to the stables he found the Inspector standing in the courtyard, gazing up at the night sky. The moon was high and Titus had not seen so many stars since they left the country.

'Such a clear night will be a cold one,' Pilbury said. 'Are you warm in the stables?'

'The straw is enough.'

Pilbury looked at him for a moment and then back up at the sky.

'I am sorry if I was sharp with you in there. You did nothing to deserve it.'

'Not at all, sir.'

'It can be an eerie business, this detecting, and I was very glad of your help when the young lady was ill.'

He lifted a hand and patted Titus's shoulder.

'Very glad.'

The hand dropped back to his side.

'Well, goodnight then, lad.'

At the door to the kitchen he paused, turned round and took off his waistcoat.

'Here. This might keep the chill off.'

The night's proceedings had badly affected the horses

and, before Titus could go to bed, he had to clean a wound in Leopold's flank where Beatrice had bitten him, and then clear the blood from Beatrice's split nose where she had repeatedly butted the stable door. For at least an hour Titus stroked them and sang them nursery rhymes until their eyes no longer showed the whites and the beating of their hearts was no longer visible between their ribs. As they finally began to doze he settled down on his own hard bed. Even with the stalks of the straw digging into his back and the rats scratching at the other side of the planks he felt content. The waistcoat was snug and smelled deliciously of pipe smoke and frying sausages. There was not the merest hint of honey.

# 11

# TOFFEE APPLES

The next morning Titus remembered Hannah's gift. Perhaps she didn't hate him quite so much as she made out. He took it from his pocket and squeezed it. It was soft enough to be material. Could it really be a piece of embroidery? A sampler, perhaps, or some Bible quotation to remember their parents by? Eagerly he tore open the package.

It was her hair. Her precious hair. So much that it must have been shorn almost to the scalp, and all held together by a noose of oakum. It slipped from his fingers and flopped into his lap.

Inside was a note. Thanks to him, and in the teeth of her strident opposition, Hannah could just about spell her own name, so she must have asked one of the older girls to write it for her.

sell this and
get me owt
of here

Titus lifted the hank of hair to his face. Already it did not smell of her, but of the vinegary brown paper. Their mother used to weave it with wild flowers and tell Hannah she was a fairy princess. Hannah would sweep around and not permit anyone to remove the decoration until she was asleep and it had become crushed and limp.

Sick at heart, Titus tucked the hair into the gap behind the brick along with their mother's. It would be another week before he could see Hannah. He could not bear to think what might happen to her in that place in the mean time.

He stared out of the little window. Already a smog was coming down, drowning the soft pink of the sky in a hopeless grey.

Later that day they found another body.

It was a small boy this time, maybe four or five. Titus heard the men talking out in the yard. There must have been something in the water, they said, some chemical from the tanner's place upriver, because the body hadn't decomposed at all. Might have gone in yesterday. Couldn't have, of course: Rancer had been in prison more than a week before he was hanged, and it bore all the hallmarks of another Wigman murder.

The doctor didn't agree.

Titus was in the yard, scraping the mud off the cart's wheels, when Hadsley came into Pilbury's office.

'The boy's been dead two days at most.'

'Are you sure?' Pilbury said.

Titus went over to the other side of the carriage to hear better.

'Of course I'm sure. *My* methods are scientific.'

Titus glanced in and caught Hadsley's acid smile but ducked his head as Pilbury walked to the window.

'Looks to me like someone was so impressed with his methods they've decided to continue where he left off,' Hadsley said.

'Was there an egg?'

'Exactly the same place: back of the throat.'

'Have you told anyone about the eggs?'

'Of course not.' The doctor frowned.

'No-one but you, me and the Chief Inspector knows about them,' Pilbury said.

'Not even the judge?'

'There was no reason to bring it out at trial. We had enough evidence and it would only have provoked more salacious headlines.'

For a moment there was silence but for the rhythmic scrape of Titus's brush against the cartwheels.

'Did you get it wrong, William?' All trace of smugness in the doctor's voice had vanished. 'Was Rancer innocent?'

'No. I'm sure of it.'

'So . . . there might be an accomplice?'

Titus's hand froze mid-scrape and even the horses raised their heads from the hay buckets to fix their large brown eyes on the window.

Pilbury's reply was almost too quiet to catch.

'There might.'

Peering in, Titus saw the two men staring at one another: Pilbury, tall and lean; the doctor short and round, with little close-set eyes that glinted with intelligence.

'Don't tell anyone yet, Hadsley, about the time of death.'

The doctor raised an eyebrow.

'I'm almost sure of the culprit,' Pilbury continued, 'and to announce a fresh murder to the press could result in a mob attack. Trust me, Hadsley, please. I will make the arrest tonight.'

'Why did you not arrest this person before if you suspected him?'

Pilbury hesitated and the doctor continued, 'You do not need to answer. You ask me to trust you, and yet you have put your own trust in the dubious visions of a young girl who claims to commune with the spirits. Back when you were still using your own powers of detection, unparalleled powers I might add, *then* I trusted you. Now . . .'

The doctor sighed and took off his spectacles. Rubbing them with his handkerchief he continued, 'I know it's been hard for you, William.'

'Hadsley, please . . .'

'I understand why you went to her. God knows I might have done the same in your position. But grief is one thing, credulity and folly are something else entirely.'

He did not look at Pilbury as he picked up his hat from the desk and turned to go.

'Get some sleep, William. You look like the walking dead.'

'Marcus.'

There was no anger in the policeman's voice. The doctor paused in the doorway but did not look back.

'If I have made a mistake give me a chance to rectify it.'

The merest hint of a nod was the only sign the doctor had heard, before he walked out into the corridor and

117

shut the door behind him. Pilbury sat down at his desk and put his head in his hands.

That afternoon there was a commotion in one of the interview rooms. Titus heard shouting out in the yard and then the clang of a cell door. He'd gone into the kitchen to warm a bucket of water for the horses' wash down, when two of the men entered. They made a pot of tea and then sat down at the table. Titus lingered at the stove to find out what had happened.

'So what do you reckon then?' said the younger man.

'She's just a tart,' said the older one. 'Too drunk to know what she's talking about, and he's a lying little thief. I'm not going to take their word over the Doc and the boss.'

'They seemed pretty sure. Said they'd taken him to the bonfire at Battersea themselves. Bought him a toffee apple. Didn't you see how red his lips were when they brought him in? Like my boy's gets when he eats 'em.'

'So he had a toffee apple, so what?'

'So they don't sell 'em nowhere until Bonfire Night, and that was Thursday: the day after they hanged Rancer.'

'What are you saying?'

'I'm just saying that maybe this one wasn't Rancer.'

'Well, as far as I'm concerned,' the older one said after a pause, 'if the Inspector says it was him it was him.'

Titus picked up the bucket and left the kitchen. Outside he paused in the sunlight and breathed in the chill air. So Inspector Pilbury was lying to his men. Did he hope to catch this accomplice himself, before the press and public found out there had been a fresh killing? It seemed he'd received enough personal criticism during the first investigation, perhaps he couldn't face anymore. Well, Pilbury might think he could pull the wool over his men's eyes, but Titus was damned if he would let him face this new danger alone.

That night he had his supper in the stables, as usual, but after extinguishing the lamp he settled himself in the shadows behind the door. From here he could see across the courtyard to Pilbury's office. The lamp was lit and occasionally Pilbury's shadow would pass across the window.

The night quickly grew cold. The horses' breath billowed out to mingle with the fog rolling over the court-yard wall. If it was to be a smoggy night he would have to keep close to Pilbury, but not so close that he gave himself away. The policeman would be furious if he caught Titus trailing him.

He dozed and when he came round the lamp was burning low in Pilbury's office. Crouching near to the ground Titus sprinted across the open yard to the other side and stood with his back to the wall, then sidled along it to peer into the office. His heart sank. Pilbury had already gone and one of the other officers was occupying his desk.

But risking a second look he saw that the figure hunched over the desk was the Inspector after all. He was recognis-able only by his neat hairline and the badges on his shoulder, because the way he slouched was so unlike his normal erect posture.

He was not writing, or reading a report, but merely sat studying his hands, turning them palm up and then palm down again, as if he did not quite recognise them. Titus swallowed, his mouth suddenly dry. There was an unspoken understanding in the station that the Inspector, however brave and clever, was of a fragile disposition.

Pilbury laid his hands on the table, threw back his head and chuckled. Titus ducked down beneath the windowsill. It was there, in the silence that followed, that Titus heard weeping. Not the weeping of a maudlin drunk, but terrible, despairing moans that ended on a wrenching sob and a shuddering gasp of breath, before continuing again. They were coming from the cells. Titus remembered the commotion earlier on involving the tart and the thief. After checking that Pilbury was not about to leave – he had pushed back his chair and was now studying his feet – Titus crept along the wall around to the cells.

Through the bars Titus could see a figure, barely more than a child, huddled in the far corner, holding itself around the knees and rocking backwards and forwards. Whatever this person had done, Titus felt an overwhelming urge to offer some comfort.

He called softly through the bars, 'Hush now, don't cry. Let me go and find the duty officer and see if he will release you.'

The boy stopped weeping and looked up.

'Titus?' he croaked. Staggering to his feet he lurched across to the door.

'Stitch! What's wrong? Why are you here?'

'Charly,' he managed, gripping the bars to support himself, 'Charly's dead.'

'Charly?' Titus repeated stupidly.

'Your precious policeman hanged the wrong man!'

Spittle flew through the bars to sting Titus's cheek, and for a moment there was such rage in Stitcher's cracked face that Titus recoiled, but then Stitcher crumpled to the ground, sobbing.

Titus ran across the courtyard and through the door that led to the front desk. There he persuaded the young duty officer to lock the front door a moment and come and see to his friend.

'It was only the violence of grief,' Titus whispered as the officer peered in at Stitcher's now motionless form, curled on the floor of the cell. 'The dead child was his brother. Please, I can vouch for him. Let me take him home.'

Stitcher seemed oblivious to the opening of his cell door and was a dead weight in Titus's arms as he hoisted him upright and dragged him into the courtyard.

'Come on, mate,' Titus panted. 'We won't get far like this. Try and walk.'

Stitcher's eyes stayed closed but his legs straightened and he allowed Titus to lead him towards the gate. On the way Titus glanced into Pilbury's office. The room was empty. He swore beneath his breath.

'Right, Stitch, we're gonna have to get a move on.'

The cold air soon woke Stitcher from his stupor and he was able to tell Titus what had happened.

Charly had gone missing the day after Bonfire Night. He'd insisted on going back to the park to hunt for discarded sweets and lost coins from the previous evening. Stitcher had told him to sod off if he thought he was trekking two miles for a muddy old toffee apple, and sent the boy off alone. No-one in the house had been concerned when he did not return that night. Charly was often taken in by do-gooding old ladies, charmed by his cherubic face and flaxen hair, only to be turfed out for pilfering the silver spoons. But when he wasn't back by Friday night they grew worried and this morning he and Rosie had gone looking for him.

They found him on the beach by Lambeth Pier. He'd been pulled out of the water by a tinker couple who were in the process of stripping him of his clothes and boots. Stitcher had gone for them with a boathook and the old pair made off before they could be forced to tell what they knew.

'He looked so perfect, like a marble angel. His feet still had the marks from the lace holes of his boots what they stole off him.'

Stitcher stumbled on the cobbles, and Titus supported him.

'Even if we hadn't of taken him ourselves to the park I should've known by his face he hadn't been dead long. I've seen drowned ones plenty of times. The skin of their hands peels off like gloves when they've been in more than a couple of hours. Charly's fingers were just a bit wrinkled. If I'd have gone with him . . .'

He couldn't continue and they walked on in a silence they'd never experienced with Hannah and Charly by their sides.

'You don't have to come no further,' Stitcher said at the turn into Orchard Street. 'I'll be all right.'

Titus reached out and touched his friend's shoulder and felt it trembling.

'Charly would think I'm a right nancy if he could see me like this, eh?'

Titus shook his head. 'Charly thought the sun shone out of your arse.'

Stitcher looked away and when he looked back his eyes were shining, but with as much fury as grief.

'I tell you what, if your useless bloody boss can't catch who killed him then I'll do it my bloody self. And when I find him . . .'

The knife flashed out from Stitcher's sleeve and, with a swift slicing movement, carved a line of blood across his palm. He squeezed his fist and let the drops fall onto the dirty cobbles.

'I swear to you, my darling,' he cried up at the starless sky, 'I'll cut his effing liver out.'

With that he turned and fled into the shadows of the darkening streets.

After taking a moment to orientate himself, Titus set off in the direction of Judas Island. Pilbury must have gone straight there to arrest the old lady.

He realised, as he made his way through the brooding alleys surrounding the old church, that a few weeks away from the place had turned him soft. He called himself names under his breath and spat a few times, but no pretence at nonchalance could prevent the hairs rising up along his spine as he stepped into the still square. A breeze had blown up and the moon fluttered briefly into view, casting mobile shadows on the ground, and washing the whole square in an eerie silver light.

The black windows of the church watched his approach. To avoid the telltale creak of the gate Titus climbed over the railing, landing in a patch of weeds that dissolved into squealing black shapes. Something wriggled and mewled under his foot – a pink, hairless thing, scrabbling at his boot with soft claws – and he hurried away from the nest before its parents regained their courage and returned.

After picking his way across the detritus towards the mouth of the church door he concealed himself just inside the porch. All was still and quiet, but for the weakening protests of the baby rat.

And then something crawled out of the darkness of the nave.

At first he thought it was some kind of giant lizard. He had seen a crocodile once in a book at school. This thing swayed from side to side as it threw out its limbs, just like a crocodile, but its movements were less fluid, more lurching. Could it be a dog? If so the thing was half dead. But it was too large to be a dog. And all the while it kept coming closer and closer, panting wheezily until it was barely a foot from the porch. It did not pause to raise its head, so perhaps it hadn't seen him. Silently he eased himself up into the empty window, where he crouched, unbreathing, as it passed beneath him and out into the churchyard.

In his relief he leaned heavily against the crumbling stone of the window, sending bits of grit and stone to patter onto the fallen leaves. The thing paused and turned its head, but only halfway, as if to listen. He knew that hawkish profile immediately.

Mrs Rancer crawled between the headstones. Occasionally a tree root or fragment of stone would overbalance her, causing her to collapse with a cry of anguish, before righting herself and carrying on. Once she'd got to the railing she hauled herself up it, grunting. Her eyes, presumably accustomed to permanent gloom, were immediately caught by the death throes of the baby rat. With considerable difficulty she bent low enough to pick it up and held it up to the moonlight.

'And what are you trying to tell me, little one?' she crooned. 'Is my faithful boy abroad once more?'

With no means of escape that did not involve blundering through the darkened church Titus watched her make her slow progress to the other side of the graveyard. The moon disappeared for a moment behind a cloud, and when it came out again she was gone. His eyes strained to make her out.

He was about to step out of the porch but stopped in his tracks, and only just managed to suppress a cry. There she was, not six feet in front of him, slithering along what remained of the path. She must have exhausted herself since she moved much slower now, giving him time to climb back up into his hiding place. As she passed beneath him the heat of her ragged breaths carried a foul smell up to his nostrils; it was coming from inside her living body but was a stench he usually associated with death – a cat had rotted in the roof of their house at Old Pye Street the previous summer and it filled the room with the same stink. In her wake, however, she left something sweeter.

Not honey this time, but flowers.

She dragged herself over to the staircase and lowered herself feet first into the crypt. Her thin white fingers were the last things to slide off the step and into the blackness. Titus waited long minutes before easing himself down from the window ledge.

No wonder Pilbury hadn't bothered to come. Mrs Rancer was too frail to overpower a house spider, let alone a healthy child. And it wasn't as if a weapon had been used to subdue the victims before drowning them. There was simply no way she could have perpetrated this murder, or the others.

He tiptoed out of the porch and began picking his way between the dark patches of undergrowth. He would go back to the station and try and get some sleep. Tomorrow night he'd have to be more alert if he was to prevent Pilbury evading him a second time.

Passing along the outside of the railing, the fragrance of flowers came to him again and, looking down, he saw the round yellow heads of tansy, forcing their way up between the nettles, some of their stalks broken halfway up.

She had been gathering flowers. What a very innocent thing for a witch to be doing in the dead of the night.

# 12

# A HEALTHY SUPPER

The morning after Titus's visit to Mrs Rancer, Inspector Pilbury arrived late for work. Titus was relieved. He hadn't slept much that night, worrying that while he'd been spying on the old woman Pilbury might have been in real danger. The Inspector was pale and drawn, though this was not unusual, but seemed otherwise himself. At lunchtime Titus offered to go to the market to give the men a change from their usual pies. The offer was taken up enthusiastically and he took orders for salt beef and cod, oysters, cheese and plum pudding. He headed down to Strutton Ground and hurried round the stalls, annoying all the wives by pushing in front of them, before finally ending up at Doctor Lovegood's Natural Remedies stall.

While the doctor was talking to another customer he glanced through the dark blue bottles. There was thousand-leaf oil for digestion, distillation of milkweed for torpor, chamomile essence for hysteria, but no sign of anything containing tansy.

'Looking for something in particular?' the doctor, now free, said, his eyes narrow.

'My mother bought some of your tansy oil,' Titus said, 'and she said it didn't work.'

The man glanced around nervously, as if to check no-one was listening.

'What did she want it for?'

'Ummm . . . a baby . . . she wanted another baby . . . Another boy.'

The doctor shook his head.

'It's not meant for that. If she'd told me she wanted that I'd've given her red clover. Tansy's for long life. This stuff, was it?'

He lifted up a bottle labelled 'athanasia'. Titus hesitated, then nodded.

'Athanasia's Greek for immortality. You sure she's not ill?'

'Umm . . . I dunno . . .'

The doctor looked uncomfortable.

'Listen, son, often people use tansy when they've got . . . a tumour. If your ma's that sick she doesn't want you knowing, well . . . Here, take this, it's for pain.'

Titus took the little bottle and thanked him.

Back at the station, the men were delighted with the respite from meat puddings, but Pilbury did not join them so Sergeant Samson sent Titus to his office with a hunk of bread and cheese. Without looking up from his work, Pilbury told Titus to have it.

In the doorway Titus hesitated. What he had seen at the Rancers' place might be important. But how could he tell the Inspector without arousing suspicion or seeming to be impertinent? Perhaps Pilbury already knew and was following other leads. He almost turned and went back to the kitchen, but something stopped him.

'Excuse me, sir.'

Pilbury raised his head and Titus was shocked to see just how thoroughly exhausted he looked.

'I was walking back through the Acre last night and I saw something curious.'

'Go on.'

'I was passing Judas Island and I happened to notice a light coming from St Mary Rouncivall. I couldn't resist a look, you know, see what the old witch was up to.' He laughed nervously. 'Her neck was huge, and she could hardly move and she was moaning a lot and, well, sir, I think she's ill. Too ill to . . .' He tailed off.

Pilbury looked at him for a long time. When he finally spoke his voice was very low.

'Tell me, Titus, last night, at the Rancers' place, did you happen to see . . .'

Titus waited. The Inspector swallowed hard.

'. . . me?'

Titus blinked at him. Had Pilbury been there after all? Was he being told off?

'N . . . no, sir,' he stammered. 'I'm sorry if I interfered with your investigation, I was just passing and . . .'

'Not at all, Titus.' Pilbury gave the ghost of a smile. 'You know, it's the most peculiar thing, but I meant to go there last night myself, and then, this morning, I simply can't remember if I did or not.'

Titus gave Pilbury as watery a smile as the Inspector's own.

'It sounds as if she's deteriorated considerably since we last saw her,' Pilbury continued.

'She couldn't walk and she stank of sickness. She can't

have long left. She was collecting a herb: tansy. It's used for tumours, I think.'

This time Pilbury gave the approximation of a real smile.

'Quite the detective, aren't you?'

'I thought it might help, sir.'

'On the contrary, boy, it gives me a very big problem indeed,' Pilbury's voice lowered until it was barely audible, 'for if she isn't responsible, then . . .'

He tailed off. Titus stayed for a moment then went back to the stables.

Pilbury kept his door shut for the rest of the day. Titus peeped in the window now and then and saw a map spread out on the floor, marked with circles and shaded areas. Pinned to the walls were photographs, scraps of material, notes and drawings. Pilbury paced around the room like a caged wolf, never staying in one place for more than a few seconds. Two people were allowed in: Doctor Hadsley and the dredgerman who had found Charly's body. They both emerged, pale and unhappy, some time later.

It brought Titus out in a cold sweat to think his information might have led Pilbury to discount a suspect. By six o'clock he could stand it no longer. What did he know anyway? Perhaps the old woman's behaviour had all been an act for his benefit.

He knocked on Pilbury's door with his heart in his mouth. When there was no reply he quietly turned the handle, assuming the exhausted policeman was dozing at his desk. The room was empty, but for the faces gazing down at him from the walls.

Titus could not tear his eyes from them. Some were chalk white, others were nearly black or had dark patches on one cheek or the forehead. Some were preserved and wax-like, others damaged from the water; some seemed to have been gnawed by rats or eels. A note attached to one picture said, *Uncharacteristic mutilation, possible keel strike?* Titus lifted it to look underneath then wished he hadn't. In one or two of the photographs it was possible to see a notch in the hairline, where a clump of hair had been cut away. These areas had been circled.

He read some of the witness statements, from the various boatmen or mudlarks who had come upon the bodies. One boy had been found under a boat beam by an old man collecting coal.

*Tis a blessed spot,* his statement read, *where two rivers join; the Thames and the Tyburn. That's why I does me larking there. Once I found a ruby ring and lived on it for nigh on a year.*

He had signed it with an X. Pilbury had noted next to it – *Was the body deliberately wedged beneath the beam to keep it in this 'sacred spot'?*

Titus's eye was drawn to the desk by a splash of bright red. The tin he had seen previously was now open. Inside, a red ribbon was woven into a peculiar corn dolly sort of thing: made not with corn, but with hair. It was the size of Titus's hand and was shaped almost like a crucifix, except that the top part was an open oval. It had been intricately knitted, and woven into the hair were ribbons and stretches of twine and rags. But for those it would have been quite beautiful. The hair was exceptionally fine and fair, like spun gold. The lid of the box lay nearby, labelled *Exhibit A: St Mary Rouncivall, October 21st 1866.*

And then his eyes strayed to a letter, open on the desk. In the top right-hand corner, written in a rough, spiky hand, was the address: 9 Blake Gardens, Fulham, and that day's date.

DEAR INSPECTOR PILBURY,
WE RECEIVED THE NOTE WHAT YOU
 SENT YESTERDAY but I AM Afraid
LILLY will NOT be ASSISTING YOU NO
MORE IN THIS MATTER. SHE WAS
 quite UNDONE After OUR last visit,
AND CONSEQUENTLY couldN'T do NO
 WORK for Nigh ON THREE dAYS. WE
 MUST MAKE A living, Sir, AND UNTIL
you decide to REIMBURSE US to THE
 TUNE of WHAT WE MAKE REGULARLY IN
OUR PRIVATE ENDEAVOURS WE do NOT
 feel WE CAN PROVIDE YOU with hER
SERVICES (you might wANT to CONSIDER
THIS CONSIDERING AS how good shE
 PERFORMED LAST time).
YOURS REGRETFULLY,
MR FRANCIS FROBISHER, ESQUIRE,
GUARDIAN of LILLY KENT

132

And then the door banged open. Titus had been caught in the act. Pilbury stood there, carrying a plate of boiled eggs and toast.

Titus stammered and blinked, trying to think of what to say. The original reason for his visit just sounded like an excuse for spying. Pilbury's face was as hard as stone, his eyes dull.

'I am sorry to intrude, sir,' he managed finally, 'but I need to talk to you about the old woman.'

'Out of my way.'

His voice was slurred and rasping. He thrust Titus to one side and sat heavily on the chair behind the desk, where he proceeded to attack the eggs. Titus hovered nervously. Was he drunk? Certainly drink had always given his father an appetite. Yellow egg yolk was drooling down Pilbury's beard and onto his shirt. He must have been working very hard indeed, as he smelled strongly and entirely uncharacteristically of dried sweat.

Titus moved away from him and went to stand on the other side of the desk. His fear was subsiding: the Inspector seemed to have entirely forgotten he was there.

Sergeant Samson walked past the door, then stopped and came back.

'Four eggs, is it?' he cried. 'Good to see you enjoying a healthy supper for once, sir!'

Pilbury did not look up but Samson strode away beaming nevertheless.

'I'm sorry to interrupt your meal, sir, but I reckon I might have been too hasty when I said as how she seemed too ill to hurt anyone. I know I said she was dying but perhaps Mrs Rancer is . . .'

Inspector Pilbury's head snapped up.

'Huh?'

'Umm . . . Old Mrs Rancer.'

Titus told him of his fears, and suggested that Pilbury might want to verify the old woman's state of health for himself.

When he had finished Pilbury did not seem to know what to say. His tongue crept into the corners of his mouth where the butter from the toast still glistened.

'So, er, I just wanted to tell you. And I'm very sorry for wasting your time.'

The policeman made no response.

'Mr Pilbury, sir, are you quite well?'

Pilbury grunted, his eyes glinting, darker than Titus remembered them. He turned and left the room, the hairs on his back bristling with the awareness of being watched.

As the sun sank and the fog crept in Titus watched the policemen leave one by one, until there was just a skeleton staff of beat officers and the duty sergeant. By seven o'clock the beat officers had departed on their rounds. It was a real pea-souper tonight and the courtyard was a dark sea of fog between the stables and the main building. Titus sat in the shadows, just able to pick out the fuzzy black square of Pilbury's window. Though the lamp wasn't lit he knew Pilbury was there. Every now and then a face would swim up to the window before submerging again into the darkness. Finally, when the horses were dozing and Titus's own eyelids were sinking, the kitchen door opened silently. Titus had never before seen the Inspector wearing the voluminous waxed overcoat the beat officers wore on bad nights. The collar was high enough to conceal his entire face and left just the merest sliver of shadow between it and the brim of his hat. For a moment two pinpricks glinted in that shadow and Titus kept very still, but they passed over him and Pilbury made for the gate.

There was every chance, of course, that he was heading straight home to bed.

Pilbury used his own key to unlock the gate, looked left and right, and then disappeared into the night. Titus scrambled up and went after him, then swore as he found the gate locked, and had to run back to fetch his key. By the time he had closed and locked the gate behind him, Pilbury was nowhere to be seen.

He might have gone to the river to look again at the site where the body was found, or he might be making for the Acre, either to the Rancer place or to interview witnesses. Titus was pretty sure the tide was in, meaning that the beach would be submerged, so at the end of King Street he took a right into Broad Sanctuary and then left into Great Smith Street, which would take him around the eastern edge of the Acre. It was a good job he knew his way around because the fog was too thick to see to the other side of the road. The carriages crawled down Broad Sanctuary, wheels scraping along the kerb and bad-tempered passengers complaining they would be late.

The first pub he came to was the Horse and Groom. He recognised a man and his son standing outside.

'Seen any coppers out?' he called to them.

'Can't see much at all tonight,' the man said. 'Why? What you been up to?'

'Nothing I wouldn't tell me mother,' Titus called, moving on, and the man laughed.

At the corner of Great Peter Street Titus turned and entered the slum.

As he moved through the alleys he became lighter on his feet, his hands curled into fists and his eyes catching every movement. He missed Hannah's presence at his side, comforting and worrying him in equal measure. It struck him that this was the first time he had thought of her in days.

He heard a child's voice calling and, as he turned into St Anne's Lane, he came upon a girl who had lived a few doors down from them in Old Pye Street. Her face was drawn with hunger and anxiety.

'What's the matter?' he asked her.

'I've lost me brother. I only went round the back of the pub for a pee and when I came back he was gone.'

Titus could think of no words of reassurance.

'I've come from the east and I never saw him,' he said quickly. 'You go up Perkins Rents and I'll keep going along the Lane.'

She nodded and they were about to split up when a piercing scream cut through the night. The girl's hands flew to her mouth and Titus set off at a run in the direction of the cry.

They found the child squatting in the gutter, his arms folded across his face. The girl flew to his side.

'What's the matter, Silas? Are you hurt?'

He was sobbing so much he could barely get the words out.

'A rat . . . pinched . . . me carrot . . .'

Her eyes widened in astonishment, and then she wrenched her little brother's arms down and used them to shake him until his whole body waggled like a Jack-in-the-box.

'What did I tell you about stayin' where you was? I've a good mind to drown you meself! An' where did you get a bloody carrot from anyway . . .?'

Titus left her cussing him and their voices were quickly swallowed by the thick air.

He was just beginning to lose his bearings when he came upon the higgledy-piggledy line of houses that led down to Judas Island. It soon narrowed into the claustrophobic alleyway he had walked with Inspector Pilbury, and he was just about to step out into the square when he saw a figure standing motionless a few yards from him. The overcoat made him look larger, but it was definitely Pilbury. His gaze was fixed on St Mary Rouncivall.

Why did he hesitate? Why didn't he go straight down and see her for himself?

Pilbury stepped forward one pace, then stopped and gave a low whistle. For a few minutes there was silence. And then the whistle was answered.

The policeman turned and walked straight towards Titus. For some reason he felt a stab of fear. He scrabbled back along the greasy brickwork of the passageway until his hands found a door: locked. Pilbury was in the passageway now, he could hear the rasping of the older man's breath echoing off the walls.

He slid past another door, then a window. Pilbury was close enough that Titus could smell his sweat in the stale air. Then suddenly he toppled backwards. The glassless window frame had crumbled behind him. The wood was so rotten it barely made a sound as he somersaulted through, to land flat on his stomach on the other side.

The flapping of the Inspector's overcoat as he passed by was like the wings of a bat.

Titus lay on the earth floor, breathing heavily. Had Pilbury confided in a colleague after all: the one he had whistled to and who he'd now left waiting on the other side of the Island to keep tabs on the old lady? This should have reassured Titus, but it didn't. It must have been the peculiar acoustics of the Island, but the second whistle sounded muffled, as if it was coming from low down, perhaps even below ground.

He got to his feet, keeping to the shadows away from the window. After a minute or two's silence from the alley outside, he crept over and peered out. It was empty. He threw his left leg over the sill, which disintegrated beneath him to leave just the crumbling bricks. As he lifted his right leg over his body swung round and he found himself looking into the room in which he had hidden. It was filled with people, crouching in the darkness. A baby crawled towards him – no, not a baby, babies were plump, this was a tiny old man – the bones jutting from his buttocks. He reached into his pocket and found the bread and cheese Pilbury had given him, but as he drew it out the sea of faces advanced and the baby was engulfed. He left them fighting over it and went after Pilbury.

He'd imagined it would be easy to get back on the Inspector's trail, knowing the streets so well, but there was no sign of him, almost as if the policeman knew the Acre better than he. He ran as fast as he could, his head snapping left to right, catching flashes of empty alleys and yards where men leaned and children played in the dirt. And then suddenly he was back where he had come in, outside the pub. He nodded to the man and his son and ran on, planning to cut back into the Acre at the junction of Old Pye Street.

'You still looking for coppers?' the boy called after him. 'Yeah.'

'I seen one not five minutes ago, tall feller in a big black coat. He was heading thataway.'

He waved an arm in the direction of Broad Sanctuary and the river. Titus thanked him and struck out in the direction he pointed.

The fog was getting thicker. On Broad Sanctuary the carriages had stopped altogether and the drivers were huddled in little groups, smoking. More than once Titus stumbled into walls or off the kerb. Approaching the bridge from the northern side he saw a dark shape moving quickly along the opposite side of the road. It was tall enough to be Pilbury, and the speed with which it approached the bridge marked it out from the rest of the night's traffic. Most of the pedestrians crept carefully, or had simply abandoned their plans and settled into the nearest pub to sit out the worst of the smog.

The shadow was growing larger and darker now as it crossed the street, heading for where Titus stood.

He paused at the corner to let it pass and start descending the steps to the beach. As he did so the figure turned slightly and Titus faltered a little. Perhaps it wasn't Pilbury after all. This person seemed to be very fat.

Once he had heard the man's feet on the pebbles below he went down after him. Stepping off the last rung he heard a peculiar high-pitched mewling that seemed to be coming from beneath the bridge. It sounded almost exactly like the squeals of the dying rat at St Mary Rouncivall, and he wondered if the man was a rat-catcher checking his traps. It was a funny place to set one, but at least he would be certain of corpses to use in attracting trade.

He followed the direction of the sound, keeping his hand in contact with the slimy wall so as not to lose his bearings. As he drew closer he could hear a voice, deep and guttural: not Pilbury's, he was sure. He almost turned to go, but the mewling sound disturbed him.

Holding both hands out in front of him, Titus stepped away from the wall and into the swirling fog. Beneath his feet the pebbles turned to sand, and then sludge.

He stopped.

Not six feet from him the figure stood by the water. He had removed the overcoat. The epaulettes on his shoulders glowed silver in the darkness.

Not a rat-catcher, then.

A policeman.

The man seemed very tall and broad, but this might simply have been due to the way he was standing, his back braced, both arms raised, palms out towards the water. He was muttering some kind of prayer, repeating the same thing over and over. After three rounds of the chant Titus thought he had made out the words.

*'Hail, spirits of the sacred river. From one who has passed beyond the lower nature, accept this gift of purity, and in return cleanse corruption from thy servant.'*

The prayer stopped. The man reached into his pocket and drew out a jar. Taking off the lid, he scooped out the glutinous contents and threw it out across the river. It sailed in a single languorous strand, to splash heavily in the water.

'*Accept this gift . . .*'

Titus dropped to his haunches and crept forward. That smell again: honey.

The man crouched to clean his hands in the shallows then straightened. Now he took something else from his pocket: round yellow flower heads that he crushed in his fist, before letting the petals scatter on the water.

'*Accept this gift . . .*'

Finally he drew out an egg. It was a boiled egg, for he bent and gently cracked the shell on a stone before peeling it off and scattering the pieces across the waves.

'*Accept this gift . . .*'

Then he turned. Titus flung himself sideways and the policeman's steps must have passed within inches of his own outstretched legs. He waited a split second then crawled after him.

Eggs. Tansy. Honey.

Did they have some meaning that Titus didn't understand?

The apothecary had explained that tansy stood for immortality. An egg must surely represent new life. And what of the honey? Aside from its sweetness the only thing that occurred to Titus was that his mother had once applied it to his foot when he trod on a rusting nail.

He followed the crunching sound of the policeman's feet and soon the huge grey slab of the embankment wall loomed into view. The figure was bending over a dark mass that must be the overcoat. One arc of a pair of handcuffs gleamed in the left-hand pocket. The coat lay on the gravel near an arch from which a muddy stream flowed down the beach to join the river. This must be the Tyburn, the river that flowed beneath Old Pye Street.

Titus had almost forgotten the rat's mewling but as the policeman approached the wall it began again and Titus realised that it was coming from beneath the coat. At the same moment he realised that the man was not fat at all, but must have been concealing something large beneath the garment.

The overcoat writhed as the footsteps drew closer. The man began to sing a lullaby:

'*Lavender's green, dilly, dilly, Lavender's blue,*
*If you love me, dilly, dilly, I will love you.*'

The garment thrashed and the mewling became a strangled scream. The policeman flung the coat aside. A child's face stared up, eyes bulging. Its mouth was open but filled with something, its hands and feet were bound. It struggled wildly as the policeman knelt beside it.

Titus cried out as a blade flashed in the moonlight and his cry was drowned by the squealing of the child. But the knife swept past its throat and up to its hairline. In the moonlight the grubby hair looked grey but, in fact, the child must have been almost as fair as Hannah. The policeman snipped off a lock of hair and tied it with a length of twine from his pocket then he lifted the child and slung it onto his shoulder.

Titus leaped to his feet.

'Stop! Murderer!'

The man stopped, his back to Titus. Voices drifted

down from the bridge above. 'Hello down there! Are you having a lark?'

Titus bent and picked up a brick.

'Put him down or I'll knock your brains out.'

'Hello . . . o . . . o!' sang the voices above. 'Is someone being murdered down there?'

The figure did not move. Titus took a step forward and raised the fist holding the brick.

'I mean it. I have a pistol.'

'Hold up! I'm coming down!' an upper-crust male voice called down from the bridge.

'Oh for goodness' sake, Simon, we'll be late,' a woman complained.

Finally the figure turned.

The brick fell from Titus's hand and struck him on the shoulder. He barely felt it. Sensing its chance the child gave a final convulsion, flipped itself onto the sand and began to crawl away on its stomach.

Inspector Pilbury glanced down at the retreating child then he turned his gaze on Titus. The eyes that burned into him were full of loathing, frustration and rage, but absolutely no recognition.

Without a word he scooped up his coat and disappeared into the fog.

A man in a tailcoat blundered into view, but caught his foot on a wooden strut and went sprawling onto the beach. He described his mishap to those above, to peals of laughter, and seemed to have trouble getting up.

'See to the child!' Titus said, before setting off after Pilbury.

He splashed through the stream and under the bridge,

but the fog was so dense and his heavy, oversized boots made him clumsy and slow. He thought he could hear Pilbury's footsteps ahead of him until the river bent westwards at Vauxhall Bridge, but here the shore became rocky and he sheered his ankle several times until it twisted badly and he could go no further.

And there he stayed on the rocky beach, as the river twisted away from him, rolling silver, rolling black, until the incoming tide covered his boots.

# 13

# SILKWORMS AND SPIDERS

Sergeant Samson kicked him hard in the shins.

'Get up! You stable boys are all alike, lazy tykes the lot of you! The coach is needed in— Good grief,' he peered down at Titus's face, 'what's the matter with you?'

Titus sat up and began folding away the blanket.

'You're a distinctly peculiar colour, boy.'

'Just a stomach upset.'

'Stay out of the kitchen, then, we don't want to go the same way.'

'Yes, sir.'

'The coach needs to be ready by nine.'

'Yes, sir.'

When Samson left, Titus got up and went into the courtyard. It was a fine day with a light breeze and in the far western corner he found a little patch of sun to stand in and let the sweat dry off him.

He ached all over from shivering. He would leave today, straight after he'd prepared the carriage. Pick up Hannah, get on a train and leave the city. Heaven knew what they would do then. It would soon be winter and too cold to sleep outdoors, but perhaps they could survive for a while sleeping in barns and begging food from farmers' wives.

The policemen were all in the kitchen tucking into eggs and bacon. Samson said something to the others and they all turned round and grinned at him, then made dramatic puking impressions. Titus raised his hand but could not force a smile to his lips. As he watched, Pilbury entered the room. He must have asked what the joke was, for a split second later he turned to look out of the window. Their eyes met and Titus was fastened to the spot. A smile spread over Pilbury's face and for a moment Titus's blood ran cold. But it was not a smile of triumph or threat; it was the same kind, weary smile Inspector Pilbury often wore.

The patch of sunlight disappeared behind a cloud and a chill crept over Titus's damp skin. And then the door opened.

'Come in, son! Don't listen to that old curmudgeon.'

'N . . . no, sir, I'd better not.'

'Very well, please yourself, but there's plenty here if you get your appetite back.'

The door closed, and Titus breathed again. For the next twenty minutes he concentrated all his efforts on ensuring that the carriage was so well prepared that none of the police officers would have cause to speak to him again. After it had left and Pilbury had gone back to his office, Titus slipped out of the gate.

He ran all the way to Little Almonry and pushed his way past the queue already forming outside the porter's office. Once inside he told the porter that he wanted to take Hannah immediately and, after an agonising wait while paperwork was filled in, Titus was allowed through to the courtyard. Hannah was playing hopscotch with some much smaller girls, giggling as the stone rolled under the skirts of a hatchet-faced female guard.

'Hannah!'

She raised her head: for a moment her face lit up before she swiftly rearranged it into a scowl. She ambled over, her gaze averted. When she was within touching distance he grabbed her arm and pulled her close.

'We gotta go,' he hissed into her ear. 'Now. Tell the nurse and go get your stuff.'

'I ain't got no stuff,' she said, frowning and pulling away. 'They burned me clothes. What you done now?'

'I haven't done nothing.'

'Lost your job?'

'I haven't lost it. It's just . . .'

She stared at him, her eyes even wider now that her face had become so thin and drawn.

'Mr Pilbury's sick.'

She gasped.

'How sick? Not . . . dyin'?'

'No, no. Sick in his mind. I think he might be dangerous.'

He began leading her towards the door to the porter's office.

'We can go to the country, maybe try and find some of Mother's relatives. It's still warm enough to sleep in barns and . . .'

She stopped and shook her arm free.

'You're just gonna leave him?' she said.

He blinked at her.

'Didn't you hear me? He's dangerous.'

Even as he said it he knew how the words sounded and

he straightened his back a little. Sure enough there was disappointment in her eyes.

'After all he's done for us?'

'What d'you want me to do?' he hissed. 'I'm not a doctor, am I? I can't help him.'

But as he spoke he realised the opposite was true. He was the only one who *could* help. If he left, it wouldn't be long before Doctor Hadsley called Pilbury to account and the new murders were broadcast to the country. Then it was only a matter of time before he was apprehended and hanged. If Titus remained, perhaps he could somehow protect Pilbury from himself. It was not as if he hadn't dealt with such outbursts of insanity before, from his father. Whatever happened, Titus had never for a moment stopped loving his father, always knowing it was the sickness of his mind not an evil nature that made him that way. He would never have abandoned him. Was he simply going to abandon his friend in his time of greatest need?

'If I go back, you'd have to stay here.'

The cries of the children echoed around the bleak walls. Somebody must have cheated at hopscotch, for a fight had broken out. Two of the girls had dragged the bonnet off a third and were clawing at her hair. The guard pounded over and tore them apart, swiping at them with the back of her hands until they subsided into sobs.

'Very well,' Hannah whispered.

'You'll stay here?'

She gulped and nodded. 'For Mr Pilbury. If you promise to help him.'

He looked at her poor, thin, bruised face: at the scratches on her cheek, the sores clustering in the corners of her mouth, the tufts of her shorn hair poking out from under the bonnet. Then he took her face in his hands and kissed her softly on the forehead.

'You are the bravest girl in the world,' he said.

When he pulled away from her there were tears coursing down her cheeks.

'I will find a way to make him better,' Titus said, his voice thick, 'and then I will come for you. I swear it will not be much longer.'

She nodded blindly.

'You do believe me, don't you?'

She nodded again, then turned and began making her way back to the little group of children. As she walked away from him she seemed to diminish, until she was as frail and insubstantial as a ghost. One of the other girls cast him a sour look and tried to put an arm around her but Hannah shook her off, picked up the stone and resumed the game.

Since he'd left his gate key in the stable, expecting not to return, Titus had to go back past the main desk. Sure enough, there was trouble.

'Where the hell have you been?' snapped the duty officer. 'Samson's on the warpath. They couldn't get the carriage in. Inspector Pilbury himself had to go and find a key.'

Titus ducked his head and hurried down the corridor that led past the offices. Samson stepped out in front of him.

'Now you listen here . . .' he began.

'He's back then, is he?'

The hair down Titus's spine prickled as he felt the Inspector's presence behind him.

'Wants a damn good hiding, sir, if you ask me.'

Then two large hands gripped Titus's shoulders and effortlessly turned him.

For a moment he could not look up. His heart was a hammer striking an anvil. He was tempted to whisper – *Let me go or I'll tell* – but could not unclench his teeth.

'It's not like you to vanish like that. We were worried.'

Samson snorted.

Finally Titus swivelled his pupils up and met Pilbury's gaze. He opened his mouth and stuttered out a few syllables, then fell silent. He scrutinised the Inspector's face, looking for some message of threat or conspiracy, but Pilbury's gaze was troubled only by concern.

'Come into my office.'

Ah, so that was why . . .

The policeman shut the door behind them and Titus waited, staring blindly at the empty desk, for whatever fate Pilbury had decided for him. A poker lay by the fire. If he could get to it he might be able to defend himself. Although there wasn't much point. If he killed or injured Pilbury he would hang – what was a slum rat's word against a police inspector's? The best he could do was lull Pilbury into a false sense of security then go to Doctor Hadsley. Surely the doctor would do everything in his power to keep his friend from the gallows, although arguably sending him to Bedlam was worse . . .

Finally Pilbury turned.

'This might seem a peculiar question, Titus, but were you awake late last night?'

'Yes, sir.'

'Do you happen to recall what time I left?'

Titus swallowed.

'Your . . . er . . . usual time, sir.'

Titus's mouth went dry as he waited for the leer or wink that would mean the Inspector knew his game. None came. And now that he thought about it he was sure that last night Pilbury had not even recognised him. That was strange in itself: surely it hadn't been that dark? Could the mental aberration that had caused Pilbury's actions come on suddenly and then just as suddenly pass? After the fit had ended was he back to being the same old Pilbury, with no knowledge of what he had done? This made Titus feel considerably better. If this was the case he could try and help his friend without guilt, and surely the authorities would not hang a man for a fit of madness he could not later recall?

Pilbury took a deep breath.

'Good, good. Thought so. Memory isn't what it used to be at my age, you know!'

He laughed but it was a hollow sort of laugh.

'Now, Samson's cross with you but I'm prepared to give you another chance, so long as my poor memory stays between you and me, eh?'

'Of course, sir,' Titus said.

He went back to the stable and lay on his back, staring up at the rafters. A spider was spinning an intricate web in one of the corners. Then it lowered itself down on a strand of silk and scuttled away under a sack.

*Silkworms and spiders.*

The phrase was from a poem he'd been given at school

for reading practice. One of the older boys had told him it was about laudanum. He'd seen plenty of drug addicts in his time. There were several opium dens in the Acre: run by Chinamen, they lent an exotic, almost opulent, air to the shabby little back streets down which their furtive clients crept. Young gentlemen, usually, although if they continued with the habit they soon came to resemble walking corpses. He'd watched with fascinated horror the decline of a pianist from a nearby garret, whose music became ever more erratic and wild, until finally it ceased altogether when the poor man hanged himself from the rafters. Now he thought about it, Pilbury's symptoms fitted perfectly with an addiction to the drug: the mood swings, the lack of appetite, the pallor, the personality change, the memory loss. Often the drug use started with a personal tragedy (the pianist's brother had eloped with his fiancée) – hadn't Pilbury supposedly lost his wife?

When Titus went back across to the station he found that luck was with him. The senior officers had gone for lunch in a club, to celebrate the birth of Samson's first grandchild. It was easy enough for Titus to slip inside Pilbury's office unobserved and close the door behind him. There he began ransacking the place.

He picked the locks of the desk drawers and riffled through the contents, searched in and under the wardrobe and examined the upholstery of the chairs. He delved into the bin but found only tobacco ash, a whisky bottle and the letter from the medium. He tested the floorboards for any loose ones. He even poured out the coal scuttle into the fireplace then replaced each coal one by one. He looked behind pictures and lifted the rug.

But after half an hour of painstaking work, he had discovered no bottle or vial. Though the room was cold he was sweating with anxiety that Pilbury would return at any moment, his mood darkened by alcohol. He turned a slow circle in the middle of the floor and tried to think where he himself might have hidden such a secret.

He thought of the little bundles of hair tucked away behind the brick in the stable.

As he bent to examine the stones around the fireplace he saw immediately a dark outline where the mortar had separated from one of the bricks. He tried to tease it out with his fingernails but it was no good, he would need a tool.

He grabbed a letter opener from the desk.

As he jiggled the blade in the keyhole he heard a hubbub coming from the front of the station. The officers were back.

Stabbing the blade into the crevice he leaned his whole weight on it, praying it would not snap, and the stone finally gave. Samson passed by outside the door and as his drunken bellowing receded Titus could hear Pilbury talking to the duty officer. He had a few moments more. Once the stone had eased a quarter of the way out he withdrew the letter opener and hurried back to the desk to replace it. Returning to the fireplace he could hear Pilbury's footsteps in the corridor. He drew out the brick and reached into the hole. But instead of a bottle of laudanum, his hand closed around something soft. He drew it out.

Confusion froze him to the spot.

He was holding a lock of Hannah's hair.

The door opened and Pilbury entered.

'Hello. What's this? What are you doing in here?'

Titus's fist closed around the hair and with his other hand he took a shovelful of coal.

'I wanted to get a fire going for you, sir, so the room was warm when you came in.'

To his ears, still ringing with shock, his voice sounded stiff and unnatural.

'Good lad. Well, carry on. I might have a bit of a doze while we're nice and quiet.'

Titus finished laying the fire, replacing the brick as he did so, then crept from the room.

When he got back to the stables he took his own parcel of Hannah's hair from the niche in the wall and compared it to the lock from Pilbury's office. They were not quite the same. Hannah's hair was finer and straighter, and it struck Titus that this lock might have belonged to Charly. All the victims he had seen on Pilbury's walls were very fair. Which word had Pilbury used on the beach: 'Purity'?

That afternoon Titus managed to replace the hair and steal a truncheon, before settling back in his spot by the stable door. From here he could observe Pilbury, armed, and subdue him if he had to.

But tonight all was well and Pilbury was on his way home, utterly himself, by eight.

The same happened the next night, and by the following day Titus's anxiety had receded a little, so that evening, when Pilbury cooked himself a large plate of bacon and eggs, Titus thought nothing of it.

Until the singing started. It was so low that he would not have heard it if he hadn't been listening.

He tucked the truncheon down the back of his

trousers, took a coil of rope from the stable door and let himself into the darkened kitchen. The ticks and creaks of the range set his nerves on edge even before he reached Pilbury's office. The door was closed and the singing inside continued. He stood outside long enough to hear the end of the song, before finally knocking.

'Come in,' a sly voice said.

Titus withdrew his hand. This was not what he had expected.

'Inspector Pilbury?' he called quietly through the door.

'Y-e-e-s-s,' the voice drawled. 'Come in, if you please.'

Titus had expected a straightforward fight during which he would try to overpower Pilbury and tie him to the chair while the fit passed, but it seemed as if this madness was not so straightforward. Pilbury's personality seemed to have split in two. Was this the one who had attacked the child on the beach? If so, might he yet recognise Titus? He thought for a moment, then leaned forward and spoke through the door.

'You must come quickly, sir, to the cells, one of the prisoners is ill.'

He already had his back turned when the door opened and he felt the strangeness of the presence on his heels as he led the way down the corridor towards the front desk. If he needed more proof, Pilbury made no protest that this was not the most direct route to the cells.

On the way past the front office he took the ring of keys that hung beneath the desk, with a nod to the duty officer, as if he was acting on Pilbury's authority.

'Evening, sir,' the man said to Pilbury and Pilbury replied likewise.

They passed out into the courtyard with the line of cells on their left. In the last few minutes a fog had rolled in and its fingers curled around Titus's feet.

'The drunk they brought in at three was making some terrible choking noises, and I was afraid he'd swallowed his tongue.'

'I see.'

'Take a look for yourself, sir, in here.'

Titus opened the cell door, leaving the key in the lock. It was as black as hell inside. Pilbury walked past Titus and into the shadows. Immediately Titus swung the door shut behind him and turned the key. At the clang of the door Pilbury spun round and his white face hurtled up out of the gloom. Titus jerked back as reeking spittle struck his face through the bars.

'You!' he snarled.

The eyes glittered, darker than Pilbury's, and the breath smelled as if it was just released from a grave.

'You deprived me of a child. Let me out or I will send you to the bottom of the river instead.'

'Mister Pilbury,' Titus said loudly. 'Please try and fight this sickness. Can you hear me, sir?'

Pilbury chuckled, a sound like the creaking of an old ship.

'Let me out,' he hissed.

Titus took a step forward, holding his gaze without flinching.

'I won't let you out, and you'll keep your trap shut unless you want to be hanged.'

'Hah!' Pilbury cried. 'That's no more painful than a wasp sting. And I should know.'

He leered through the bars and Titus backed into the courtyard. Soon the monstrous grin was drowned in smog, but even when he had reached the sanctuary of the stables he felt he could still see it floating towards him through the fog.

After an initial bout of bellowing and door-rattling the cells stayed quiet for the rest of the night, but Titus lay paralysed with fear until dawn finally broke.

As the fog burned off Titus forced himself up and out into the courtyard, fully expecting to see the cell door broken open. It was still padlocked. He took the key he had slipped from the bunch before returning it to the desk last night, and went over to the cell. Pilbury lay on his side on the floor breathing deeply.

Titus knocked quietly.

'Mister Pilbury?'

The figure stirred and as it stretched its legs the tang of urine drifted across to Titus. But that was all. There was nothing of the grave in the foetid air of the little room.

'Inspector?'

The eyes opened, blinking in the sunlight.

'Do you know me, sir?'

'Titus? Is that you?'

Titus hurriedly unlocked the door and helped Pilbury to his feet.

'What happened? Why am I in the cells?'

There was fear in his voice.

'Let me take you back to your office.'

There was a spare pair of trousers in Pilbury's wardrobe and while the Inspector dressed Titus went to fetch a bottle of brandy from the Rose and Crown. When he came back Pilbury was leaning on his desk, his head in his hands.

He looked up when Titus entered and Titus marvelled at the difference between the Inspector now and what he had been last night. Certainly he could never mix them up. Pilbury's eyes were set in deep wells of grey and criss-crossed with scarlet but they were not those monstrous black pits from the night before. He was trembling as he took the brandy and swigged it straight from the bottle.

As he drank, Titus talked rapidly.

'Last night you said you wanted to look in on one of the prisoners, and you asked me to come as the fellow was violent. We found him asleep. You said you wanted to discuss the Rancer murders with him and that you'd wait until he woke up. I can only think that you fell asleep wait-ing and whoever was on duty didn't see you on his rounds and locked the door by mistake.' He ended with a shrug and a reassuring smile. 'You have been very tired, sir.'

But the Inspector was not reassured.

'I remember nothing after five. I pissed myself, boy.'

Titus looked at his boots.

'There is something gravely amiss. I shall ask Hadsley to come and examine me. And Titus, I must ask you again not to tell the others . . .'

'I won't, sir.'

For a moment Pilbury's mouth trembled but he quickly recovered himself.

'You are a good lad. Now, off with you. Beatrice and Leopold will be wanting their breakfast.'

# 14

# CHARLY

The following evening Titus watched Pilbury, bent and sunken-eyed, trudge out of the back door at five and hail a cab home.

But after the Inspector left, Titus just couldn't settle. He wandered about the station, eventually ending up at the front desk where the duty officer let him sit behind the counter and read the evening edition. A little later on a delivery boy came in.

'Package for Inspector Pilbury,' the boy said, 'from Doctor Hadsley.'

'The Inspector's gone home,' the duty officer said. 'Can you take it on to him?'

'Nah. Me mother's expecting me back to help with the baby.'

'There's a penny in it if you do.'

'And a thrashing from me mother. No thanks.'

He turned and scurried out of the door.

'I'll take it,' Titus said. 'I don't suppose you'll need the cart before the pubs close.'

The duty officer agreed and gave Titus an address in Chelsea. He walked down Victoria Street then cut through the back streets behind the station to Eaton Square. The gang often used to come up here in the small hours and dare one another to try and break into one of the vast houses. But these were the properties of politicians and lords, and Stitcher and Co. were not yet desperate enough to risk their necks. His steps slowed and he gazed into the lighted windows where families sat around sumptuous drawing rooms, or dined beneath glittering chandeliers. It wasn't the glitz and opulence that drew his eyes, however, it was the child reading on his father's knee in one house; the girl playing the piano while her family looked on in another; the crying baby in its mother's arms.

He gazed through the railings until frowning servants whisked the drapes closed and the scenes vanished.

Passing through Sloane Square onto the King's Road, Titus tried to ignore his itchy fingers as he went past shop after shop of fine jewellery, perfume, leather gloves, confectionery, and all the other wonders that were a world away from the Acre.

Shawfield Street was a wide terrace of three-storey, white-stucco houses with black railings and polished brass on the doors. Number twelve had three black-and-white chequered steps that led up to a dark green door. On this door, he noticed, the brass was a little tarnished. He rapped three times then took a step back to wait.

After three or four minutes had passed he pressed his ear to the door. There were no sounds of movement inside.

The shutters of the front room were closed. Did that mean Pilbury hadn't been home since early this morning?

A flame of fear sprang up in his chest.

He knocked again, harder and longer, then stepped

back onto the street and tried to see into the upper windows. The shutters upstairs were closed too.

Perhaps it was nothing more serious than that Pilbury had stopped for a drink somewhere. Titus had specifically heard Pilbury telling the cabbie to bring him back here so he could not be far away. Unless it had been a ruse . . .

Titus was sitting on the steps, wondering what to do, when a woman's skirts appeared in his field of vision.

'Hello, my darling. You waiting for Mr Pilbury?'

A short round woman stood before him carrying a basket.

'Yes,' Titus said, getting to his feet, 'I've a delivery for him. But he's not in.'

The woman laughed. 'Oh, I'm sure he is.'

She took a key from the pocket of her apron and climbed the stairs.

'I'm Dorothy Membery, his housekeeper. Well, former housekeeper he calls it, but I still look after him as much as he'll let me – a cake or a pie now and again to keep his spirits up.'

She opened the door and stepped into the darkened hallway. 'Come in and I'll see if I can find him for you.'

Titus followed her down the hallway to a kitchen at the end. This room was lighter as it backed onto a large garden whose flower beds were crowded with brightly coloured blooms and weeds in equal measure. There was a small glass-house against the western wall but instead of plants it seemed to contain only tools and blocks of wood. He could just make out, on one of the worktops, a ball and two short sticks.

'It's a shame, isn't it?' Mrs Membery said, coming to stand beside him. 'To let it go to ruin. But it was her garden and he won't let no-one else touch it.'

She went back to the table and began unloading the basket.

'Beef and oyster pie,' Mrs Membery announced. 'That's his favourite. Roast shoulder of mutton, and a jam sponge.'

Titus's stomach growled and his tongue prickled at the sight of the sugar-crusted cake.

'Now, why don't you go off and find him. Stairs play merry hell with my hips. He's probably in the back room at the top.'

As he was climbing the stairs she called out to him, 'Make sure he gives you your bus fare back!'

'It's all right,' Titus said. 'I can walk back to the station.'

Mrs Membery appeared in the hall. 'You work with him, do you?'

Titus nodded, feeling rather a fraud.

'Well, in that case,' she disappeared and came back with the basket, 'I'll be off. Mr Membery will be clamouring for his tea. Maybe he'll even let you have a taste of that cake . . . Cheerio!'

A moment later she was out of the door. As it swung shut, gloom descended on the hall.

Continuing up the staircase, Titus noticed patches of dark wallpaper where pictures must once have hung. Two were oval, for portraits.

The room at the top of this first flight was in darkness. He stood on the threshold and called quietly, 'Mr Pilbury?'

A shape was stretched out across a sofa. He didn't think it proper to shake Pilbury awake so he went to the window and opened a shutter.

The shape was an overcoat.

Though large and presumably light and airy when the

shutters were back, this room was being used as some kind of storeroom. A piano was almost completely disguised by leaning piles of papers. The floor was similarly covered. There were dirty plates and beer bottles on almost every surface, and the unmistakable black confetti of mice. It took him a little while to be certain there was nobody there.

Next door was a dining room. The table, a golden walnut affair with feet like lions' paws, could have seated twenty people, and was laid out with silver cutlery, which still gleamed despite the tarnish and dust. The room was so dusty it was as if Titus was viewing it through a veil. He took a step inside and his foot threw up a little cloud of dust motes that hung in the air, illuminated by the thin evening light that seeped through the shutters.

He mounted the next flight of stairs. On the next floor was the master bedroom. His eyes had got used to the darkness now and he could make out an unmade bed and piles of clothes strewn around. The musty smell of unwashed linen hung in the air and Titus passed quickly down the landing. The next door he came to was another bedroom, with rose-patterned wallpaper. These shutters were open and the sunset fell obliquely onto an iron-framed bed with a damask bedspread. There was a large black chest of drawers on top of which sat a jug and ewer, and beneath it was a square rug upon which someone had embroidered a posy of blue pansies above the word 'Welcome'. Perhaps it was because of the light but he liked this room, and walked over to the window to see what kind of a view it had. From up here the garden looked beautiful: the weeds were invisible and the grass was a lush green. By a pond at the far end perched a red-hatted gnome with a fishing rod. Titus smiled at the thought of Mr Pilbury buying himself a garden gnome. But then, perhaps it hadn't been bought for him.

As he turned to leave the room he suddenly understood what the ball and two sticks in the glasshouse were. Leaning drunkenly against the pillow was a gangly rag doll, its wooden head and arms painted pink. Pilbury had been making toys.

There was only one room left. The door was ajar and when Titus pushed it lightly with his fingertips it swung noiselessly open, as if it had been waiting for his touch. He raised his hand to shield his eyes from the full radiance of the evening sun, filling the room with a syrupy glow and making the four brass knobs on the iron cot against the wall shine.

The side of the cot had been lowered and Inspector Pilbury was curled up inside. The warmth of the sun, added to the profusion of pink in the room – wallpaper, carpet, bedclothes – gave his face a healthy glow. He seemed to be peacefully asleep, his moustache puffing up at every soft snore.

Titus wondered whether he ought not to just creep downstairs, leave the package on the table and let himself out again. But what would Pilbury think when he found it? That someone had been wandering around his house without his knowledge?

He backed out of the room, pulled the door closed, waited a few moments, then knocked loudly.

A cry came from inside.

'Mr Pilbury. It's Titus. Mrs Membery let me in. I've brought a package from Doctor Hadsley.'

There was a long time in which the only sounds were the creak of bedsprings and the rustle of bedclothes, then Pilbury appeared at the door. His hair was sticking up, his moustache was out of place and there were creases all down one cheek. He smelled of stale beer.

'Good grief, was it that urgent?' he croaked.

'I don't know, sir. Sorry to bother you, I'll be on my way.'

'No, wait. He might want an answer.'

Pilbury fumbled with the package with stiff and clumsy fingers but eventually the wrapping tore and a bottle thudded onto the carpet. He bent over to pick it up and then drew out the note.

After he'd read it he gave a chuckle and rubbed his eyes.

'Damn him,' he said, handing the note to Titus.

It read: *Something to help you sleep.*

'Well, now that I am no longer in that blissful condition perhaps you'd like something warming for your journey home. I've a good port somewhere and there may even be a clean glass or two.'

They sat in the kitchen in a silence that was both comfortable and comforting to Titus. The port was delicious and filled the hole where supper ought to be. Its heavy fragrance numbed his brain. Pilbury drank quickly: two tumblers filled to the brim were gone before Titus had got halfway through his first.

'So you met my housekeeper?'

'Yes. She was very hospitable.'

'I'm sure she was,' he snorted, 'in my house!'

'Sorry, sir. I didn't mean . . .'

'Don't worry, Titus. The poor woman was with us for years, and knew my wife from a child. She is lost without her.'

Titus's mouthful of port was more difficult to swallow. He wanted to offer some comfort or empathy to Pilbury but anything he said would sound impertinent.

'And just when I thought it could not get any worse,' Pilbury murmured, draining the dregs from his glass and pouring himself another, 'I start losing my mind. I've heard of men my age who start losing their memories: within six months they're wearing babies' napkins and being spoon-fed by their wives.' He gave a mirthless chuckle.

'No, sir,' Titus ventured, 'I'm sure it's no more than tiredness and overwork. Plus,' he cleared his throat, 'you don't seem to eat much.'

'I have been overtired, overworked and underfed before. This is different.'

The Inspector stared into the ruby liquid, swilling it around his glass. After a while Titus got up.

'I'd best be getting back to see to the horses.'

Pilbury said nothing until Titus was at the door, then he stood up unsteadily.

'I'm sorry, lad. I'm not myself tonight.'

Without his hat and coat and with shirt and hair disarrayed he looked like Titus's father.

'Yes you are,' Titus said quietly, and went out.

The station was silent and shadowy when he got back. Evidently the men were all out on the beat.

Titus crept through the darkened kitchen, pausing to slip the bread knife into his belt, before continuing on to Pilbury's office. The silent room unnerved him, its pale faces watching him from the walls. He withdrew the brick in the fireplace and took out the lock of Charly's hair, then retrieved a screwed-up letter from the bin and wiped off the ash. He tucked both into his pocket.

From the corner of King Street he could catch a bus all the way to Fulham and he managed to slip past the conductor while a fat woman struggled on. The traffic was heavy and when they got to Fulham he had time to see the street sign halfway up Harwood Road: Blake Gardens. He scrambled down the steps from the top deck and leaped off the bus.

The houses in Harwood Road were all grand five-storey affairs, but Blake Gardens was a yellow brick terrace of cottages, possibly intended for the servants of the bigger houses. They had neat little front gardens and lace curtains in the windows.

Number nine was much the same as the others, although less well cared for. The lawn was patchy, the privet brown and leafless, and the black paint on the door was peeling off in strips.

Creeping over to the window, Titus peered inside. Frobisher was sitting by the fire gnawing a chicken leg. In his other hand was the remains of a glass of beer. After glugging down the frothy dregs he thumped the glass down on the floor, tossed the chicken bones into the fire and barked, 'Lill!'

A moment later the medium came in. If possible she looked thinner and paler than the last time Titus had seen her. She took the plate and headed for the door.

'I'm going to the club. Don't use too much coal while I'm gone.'

She nodded and went out. Frobisher stood and stretched his legs. Then, after checking his pocket watch by the clock on the mantelpiece and lifting one buttock to fart, he went out.

Titus scrambled to the other side of the bay window and pressed his back against the wall of the house as Frobisher emerged putting on his top hat, and went out of the front gate.

Titus waited a minute before trying the front door. It was locked. He wondered whether to go back to the beginning of the street, scale a wall and go through all the back gardens, but in the end he gave the door a sharp rap then concealed himself once more.

A moment later the girl opened the door. There was a pause and then she stepped out onto the porch. He could see her perfectly in profile: the line of her straight nose, the barely perceptible swelling of her chest beneath the baggy dress. He held his breath and waited for her to notice him. But she didn't.

'Francis?' she called. 'Did you forget something?'

A little breeze made the dry hedge whisper and she rubbed her arm where goosebumps had appeared.

Titus eased sideways until he was under the roof of the porch.

But his caution was unnecessary for now she walked down the path and leaned over the gate. He darted into the darkness of the hall. He was lucky there were no lamps lit as he hadn't made it to the room at the end of the passage before she came back in.

While she turned her back to shut the door, he slipped into the kitchen.

Against the wall to the left squatted a large, black and fortunately cold range. He crouched down on the far side of it to wait.

From the living room came little clinks and taps as she

cleared Frobisher's plate and glass. He experienced a flash of fear when a glowing white face appeared in the window until he realised it was only the lantern she carried up the hall.

Titus watched her place the lantern on the kitchen table, drink the last few dregs of the beer, then take the plate and cup to the sink. Her face swam up in the glass and she turned on the tap. Somewhere nearby, the boiler began to groan.

Slowly he got up.

The water gushed as he crept around the table, never taking his eyes off her, though she didn't raise her own from the water. He slid the bread knife out of his belt.

She turned off the water and at the same moment he sprang forward, grabbing her around the middle and pressing the knife to her neck.

'Start summoning demons,' he hissed, 'and I'll cut your throat before you can say Abracadabra.'

Under his bicep, the little medium's heart fluttered like a bird. He could have broken her in half with one flex.

'There is no money here,' she said, 'nor any valuables. You're hurting me.'

'Promise not to scream and I'll take it away.'

'I promise,' she whispered.

Titus withdrew the blade and tucked it back into his belt.

'Sit down.'

She did as she was told and he lowered himself into the chair next to her. They regarded one another in silence until Titus began to worry that she was trying to mesmerise him with her large dark eyes. And then he worried that she might hypnotise him into stabbing himself with his own knife so he got up quickly and put it out of reach on the range.

'There now, that's much more civilised, isn't it?' he said, returning to the table.

'Who are you?'

'My name doesn't matter. Yours, I believe, is Lilly Kent, though you pretend to be a "Signorina Vaso".'

'That was Mr Frobisher's idea,' she said quietly. 'He thought it sounded mysterious. What do you want?'

Titus leaned back in his chair, making the rickety wood creak.

'I'm a friend of Inspector Pilbury's.'

He was surprised to see her relax at the name.

'How is the Inspector?' she said, with round, innocent eyes.

'You should know,' he said, 'you did it to him.'

She blinked, then frowned.

'Did what?'

He leaned over.

'Well, there's two options as I can think of,' he said, his voice low, 'one: you're a fake and you've driven him mad by some kind of hypnotising, or two: you're not a fake and you've put a demon in him.'

The lamp hissed quietly.

'I'm not a fake,' she whispered.

'Well, in that case,' he said, through gritted teeth, 'how about you tell me why you've turned him into a devil?'

'Tell me what's happened,' she said.

He frowned. Her concern seemed genuine. Was she trying to stall him until her manager got home?

'When's Frobisher back?'

'Umm . . . I don't know. Midnight possibly. Or one.'

He'd just have to take a chance on her telling him the truth and be ready to escape out of the back if he heard the front door.

'I watched you. The night you came to the station. When they brought Joseph Rancer in.'

She nodded slowly.

'You were in Pilbury's office . . .'

'We were trying to summon the child,' she said. 'The last murder victim. But she was too distressed to identify her killer.'

'You'd given up and were talking to Mr Pilbury when something . . . strange happened.'

She leaned forward, her lips parted.

'Something white came out of your mouth and went into Pilbury's.'

Lilly's breath caught in her throat.

'Are you sure it wasn't pipe smoke, or fog?'

'No, not really. I only know that since then he's been acting strangely.'

'How?'

Titus got up and went to the window. If he told her the whole story he'd be putting Pilbury in mortal danger. She was mercenary: the letter made that clear enough. If she thought she might make money out of it wouldn't she just go straight to the press, or worse, the police? He rubbed his face, then dug his hands into his pockets. The lock of hair, nestled deep down in the corner, was sleek against the back of his fingers.

'What's your name?' she said softly.

'Titus. Titus Adams.'

'How old are you?'

'Fifteen.'

'Me too.'

He turned round, leaning against the cold porcelain of the sink.

'He your uncle, that Frobisher bloke?'

'No. Although I used to call him uncle. He was my mother's friend when we lived in Somerset. He saw me having my fits, as Mama called them, and told her we could make a fortune from them. It was he who brought me to London.'

'Looks like he was right about making a fortune,' Titus said, glancing up at the high ceiling and elaborate cornicing.

'It is a nice house, but we live beyond our means. He spends so much in his club up in town that we have no money for food or fuel. That's why I have to work all the time.'

'Is that what you were doing at the station, working?'

She glanced at him sharply.

'I don't ask the Inspector for money. I try to help.'

Realisation dawned on Titus.

'But he paid you once upon a time, right?' he said. 'That's how you got to know him. He wanted you to contact his wife.'

She looked away and nodded, reddening slightly.

'Elizabeth. Grace was the little daughter. She died of typhoid and the mother went after her a few weeks later. He begged me to try and contact them but, as I expected, they had moved on to the next sphere. Untroubled spirits do not linger.'

He stared at her.

'And troubled ones? Those that died violently?'

'They find it more difficult to pass. Some become lost. Some yearn to speak to those they have left behind.'

'Some try to come back.'

Again she looked sharply at him.

'Why do you say that?'

'Inspector Pilbury is sick. Very sick.'

'Sick in spirit, you mean?'

Titus tilted his head and stared up at the demon faces made by the coiling plaster leaves. They grimaced back at him, their tongues lolling.

'The spirit is not his own.'

She got up from the table.

'Titus. Tell me what you came here to tell me.'

'I didn't come to tell you anything!' he snapped. 'I came to find out why you made Rancer's spirit possess Inspector Pilbury!'

Silence fell like a hammer. The lantern guttered and dimmed. The girl seemed to turn to stone before him, her eyes and skin and dress merging into cold grey.

'I saw him try to kill a child,' he said.

'No,' she whispered.

'There are laws against witchcraft.' He forced the words out through clenched teeth. 'If you tell anyone I will see you hanged.'

'I . . . I . . .' she stammered, then covered her mouth with her hand.

Swallowing hard, two or three times, she took the hand from her mouth, inhaled deeply and finally spoke.

'He was hanged the day before my visit to the police station, wasn't he?'

Titus nodded. 'He had a way of doing his killings. I followed Pilbury to the river and saw him doing the same. I stopped him and he ran away, seemingly without recognising me.'

'He could have gone mad. Just be copying the killer.'

'He's not mad. That's the worst part. If they catch him they will hang him for sure.'

'But he can be stopped before he kills.'

Titus shook his head slowly.

'There's been another murder.'

They stared at one another then Lilly shook her head.

'That was another Rancer killing,' she said. 'It just took a long time to find the body.'

'I knew that boy. He was alive the day after Rancer hanged.'

She began walking around the table, rubbing her arms, blinking rapidly, muttering to herself.

'I want you to contact him,' he said.

She stopped and looked at him, then sat down and put out the lantern.

Moonlight cast long, grasping shadows of the trees on the walls and table. It lit up her pale face and dress, making her glow like a ghost. Titus felt as if he was the only solid, real thing in the whole house.

'What was his name?' she said.

'Charly. I don't know his surname.'

'This will be difficult without an item of clothing.'

He swallowed, then said softly, 'I have his hair.' Reaching into his pocket he took the limp clump and handed it to her.

She took it and held it to her nose. Her face twisted a

little, as if in pain, then she closed her eyes. For a moment there was just the even sound of her breathing and the distant tick of the clock in the other room. And then her breathing quickened and her eyes snapped open.

'Piss off, you dirty great pervert!' roared a voice several octaves higher than hers. Titus's blood crawled to a standstill.

'Charly?' he managed.

'Who's that? Who said that?' said the child's voice, still too tight with fear to be identifiable.

'It's me, Titus. Your friend.'

The medium's eyes swivelled round and stared at him.

'Where's Stitch?'

Titus's breath caught in his throat. He forced himself to speak evenly. 'I've seen Stitch and he's OK. He loves you, Charly.'

'Where am I?'

'I don't know. But I think you're on the way somewhere different. Don't be scared.'

'Where? I can't see nothing. Everything's dark here.'

Calmer now, the voice had reached a more natural pitch. For a moment silence fell as the wide eyes swept around the room. Titus felt as if his own body was somewhere entirely different to the tight ball of his consciousness. He was dimly aware of his heart pounding and his blood racing but all his attention was fixed on the medium's mouth, from which his little friend's voice came, pure and unfiltered. A tear welled up in her eye. Titus leaned forward and touched her hand. It was ice-cold and slightly damp.

'Do you believe in God, Charly?'

'Yeah. Course. I tried to speak to him but he ain't said nothing back.'

'Well, I reckon he's waiting for you, but there's something that needs to be sorted out here first.'

'Yeah. That bloke. The policeman.'

Titus swallowed hard, then continued.

'What about him?'

'He held me down, under the water, till everything went black.'

'Who was it?'

Time seemed to congeal as Titus watched the girl's mouth slowly open. His eyes had turned to dry pebbles.

'That one what used to bring you and Hannah home sometimes.'

Titus's stomach dropped.

'Why'd he do it, Titus?' Charly's voice rose in pitch. 'I was so scared and the water was so cold, and I couldn't breathe and . . .'

Panic tightened his voice. Titus struggled to find the breath to soothe him.

'I'll make sure he's stopped, Charly,' he whispered, 'I promise.'

'Tell Stitcher and Rosie that I miss 'em.'

'I will.'

And then he was gone. Lilly blinked, gave a little gasp and her eyes focused on Titus.

'What did he say?'

'Didn't you hear him?'

She shook her head. 'If I allow a spirit in completely, everything is dark for me until I'm back in my own body again.'

'He said . . . He said it was Pilbury.'

# 15

# STITCHER

Titus walked back to the station. The moon was now swathed in a fog whose fingers seemed to reach out for him all the way. He couldn't shake the feeling that someone was following him and continually glanced behind and around him, but was unable to see further than the nearest lamp post.

Relief flooded over him when he saw that he was in the environs of the station and he ducked down an alley to cut off the corner.

He was halfway down, and could see the gates of the courtyard, when a hand closed over his mouth and a knife was pressed into his stomach.

From the angle of the filthy arms he guessed that his attacker was considerably shorter than him. But he was strong and trembling. This was a bad sign. If the boy was afraid then the merest sound from the street might panic him into cutting Titus's throat.

He held up his hands.

His attacker stank. He was certainly a pauper, probably an Acre kid, but if so surely he'd have recognised Titus and known the hit would be fruitless. Bold too, to pounce just yards from the police station.

'Where you been, Titus?' hissed a voice at his shoulder.

The voice was trembling, but not with fear.

Titus gave an exclamation and tried to pull the hand from his mouth but the knife pressed harder into his stomach.

'Let me explain something to you before I take me hand away. If you shout out for your mates in the station, I'll kill you. And if you don't tell me exactly what's going on, I'll kill you. If you understand then stick up your thumb.'

Titus did so and the suffocating grip on his mouth and nose was released.

'Stitch,' Titus cried, spinning round. 'What the hell—?'

He stopped when he saw Stitcher's face.

The boy looked half dead. He'd lost a great deal of weight, his skin was black with grime and there were sores around his mouth. But his eyes burned with ferocity. One of the fingers curled around the knife had slipped off the end of the handle and was clutching the blade. Drops of blood were dripping off it to splash onto the cobbles, but Stitcher did not seem to notice.

'Where you been?' he hissed again, and Titus saw there was no vestige of friendship left in him.

'Nowhere. Delivering a parcel for Pilbury.'

The punch sent him reeling on his back into the stinking puddles.

In a moment Stitcher was on him, gripping the knife with both hands, a few inches above Titus's face.

'Lie to me one more time and I'll kill you. And then I'll go back for Hannah.'

Titus stared at him. A grey string of saliva drooled from

Stitcher's mouth and down his own cheek. The boy had gone mad. But it sounded like he hadn't followed him to Lilly's. He had to protect her, and Pilbury.

'You want the truth? OK. You were right. The murders have started up again.'

Stitcher took a great gasp of air.

'I knew it!'

'I've been trying to help Pilbury . . .'

'Pilbury!' Stitcher snarled. 'I should just cut his head off now. That lying scum. He said Rancer killed Charly when he was already hanged.'

'He should've listened to you . . .'

'Too right he should've.'

The knife dropped to Stitcher's side as he wilted. There was a chance Titus might be able to snatch it from him but if he did he might have to kill his friend: the state he was in, Stitcher would try and tear him to pieces with his bare hands.

'He's looking for Rancer's accomplice now.'

Stitcher's head snapped up.

'Who is it? I wanna get to him before the police can send him off with a painless little hanging.'

'I . . . I don't know. I think he's got some leads.'

'Leads? Effing leads? What good is leads?'

Taking a deep breath Titus sat up sharply enough to roll Stitcher off him. He balanced on his haunches, ready to bolt. Stitcher sprang into a crouch, snarling like a dog.

'Leads is what the police use, all right? Now, I know you're out for blood but there's no sense killing the wrong person, is there?'

Titus slowly stood up, his eyes never leaving Stitcher.

179

'Now listen. I'm just the stable boy. They don't tell me anything. But if I do find something out I'll tell you straightaway, all right?'

Stitcher stood up too. The ferocity had gone out of his eyes, leaving only exhaustion and grief.

'I loved him so much,' he said.

'I know.'

For a moment Stitcher just looked at Titus, his whole body hanging loose, as if the bones could barely hold themselves together.

'If you keep anything from me,' he began with a sigh, 'I'll . . .'

'I know. You'll kill me. Or cut my head off.'

'That usually does it,' Stitcher said, with a wan smile, then he turned and dragged himself away down the alley.

# 16

# BOOT POLISH

The whole of the next day was spent running errands: Titus had to deliver a letter to the coroner, round up some men to take part in an identity parade, collect uniforms from the laundry, before finally heading to Covent Garden for more supplies of hay and nuts.

Beatrice and Leopold were not in the stable when he got back, which was odd, because the cart was there. But when he entered he saw them, huddled in the far corner, the whites of their eyes visible around the brown irises.

'What's the matter with you two?' he cried, rather pleased to have been so missed. 'I was only gone a while. Come on. I've got a couple of apples in my—'

He stopped suddenly when he saw Inspector Pilbury standing by his bed. In the policeman's hand was the hank of Hannah's hair from the hole in the wall. His blood ran cold as he realised how such a discovery must look to the Inspector.

'It's my sister's,' he said quickly. 'Hannah cut it off and wanted me to sell it but I couldn't bring myself to.'

But as Pilbury raised his head Titus knew he had made a terrible mistake.

'Put it down, now,' he said softly. 'Before I call one of the men.'

The policeman chuckled.

'And tell them what their precious Inspector has been up to?'

Titus opened his mouth and closed it again. Behind him the horses skittered.

Rancer's hand lifted the hair to his lips and inhaled deeply, then he tucked it into his pocket.

'You took a child from me. You'll pay me back.'

Titus reached for the truncheon but it was out of arm's length behind the door.

'Hannah. A pretty name.'

'Get out.'

'When I'm ready,' Rancer smiled.

Their eyes locked and Titus grew dizzy gazing into their bottomless blackness. Suddenly there were heavy foot-steps in the yard.

'What are you doing in there, boy!' Samson roared.

Titus looked to Rancer, expecting to see the murderer's presence recede to be replaced by the Inspector's. But it did not. Rancer's eyes were round. His lips worked quickly, he began to tremble.

He seemed transfixed with fright as the stable door banged open and Samson's huge shadow filled the opening.

'Oh, I'm sorry, sir,' Samson said, 'I didn't know you were talking to the boy. Titus, when you're done the cart needs preparing for Newgate.'

'Yes, Sergeant.'

As soon as Samson left Titus turned his attention back to Pilbury, but the spirit had vanished, leaving only the Inspector gazing about him in utter bewilderment.

* * *

After he'd prepared the cart, Titus went to Pilbury's office and asked if any of his boots needed cleaning. The boots were produced, but when Titus said he would work outside the door, Pilbury insisted he remain inside by the fire.

He began as slowly and carefully as he could, first removing the laces and laying them down on the floor, then spreading out an old newspaper he'd pulled from the kindling pile.

Pilbury sat at his desk for a few minutes then sighed, got up and said he was going to make some tea. A moment later Titus heard his voice in the kitchen. Quickly he checked behind the brick in the fireplace. The crevice contained only Charly's hair, not Hannah's.

Pilbury returned with a pot of tea, two cups and some cake. Titus immediately devoured his cake but Pilbury only sipped at the tea. When he put the cup down it clattered against the saucer.

For some time the only sound was the soft shush of horsehair on leather as Titus brushed imaginary dirt off the boots.

Pilbury got up and went over to the wall where the faces stared back at him. He took a picture down and scrutinised it, then replaced it and went back to the desk and rested his head on his hand.

'Put another log on the fire, would you?' he said.

Titus did so.

'It is getting colder, isn't it?'

'I'm not cold, sir.'

'Cold weather makes the smogs worse.'

He looked at Titus. His lips were tight and bluish.

'He only strikes in the smog,' he continued softly.

'Who, sir?'

'Rancer . . . Wait, no, Rancer is dead. Whoever is imitating Rancer. On Bonfire Night it was so thick they could barely see the fireworks.'

'There is a good wind tonight. It wou't.'

Pilbury nodded and looked away, then he shivered.

'Put another log on the fire, it's freezing.'

Though the fire blazed just inches from his back a chill crept through Titus. He had seen the Inspector angry, frustrated, morose, but never like this. Never afraid.

'It'll soon warm up, sir,' he said, but the Inspector was staring at the file on his desk.

Titus opened the tin of polish and used a rag to scoop out the gunge, black as river sludge, and slap it onto the boots. He covered each one with polish, working it into the seams and the furrow where the upper joined the sole. Then he sat back and waited for the leather to be absorb it.

The Inspector was still staring at his desk, a moment later he unlocked one of the drawers and drew out a whisky bottle.

Titus looked away. An old headline in the now smeared newspaper on the floor caught his eye.

# ANOTHER FAIR VICTIM OF FOUL MURDER.

A child's body was pulled from the river last night, the sixth in what has become a grisly series. Like the others, the girl was reputedly of fair complexion, though her flaxen hair was besmirched by river mud

Pilbury went over to the window.

'The sky is full of stars,' he said in a lighter tone. 'Come and see.'

Titus went and stood beside him. Pilbury had complained of being cold, but the heat poured off him in damp waves.

'The moon is so bright,' Titus exclaimed.

'A smuggler's moon,' Pilbury said. 'You can get up to mischief in the country on a night like this, but not in the city. A million eyes will find you out. So, be warned . . .' He smiled at Titus and the dark circles around his eyes crinkled.

'It'd be a bit daft to get up to mischief in a police station, sir, don't you think?'

The Inspector laughed loudly, and Titus could hear the relief in it.

'It's an early night for me,' he said, patting Titus's back. 'A good night's sleep is probably just what the doctor would order.'

Titus hoped this meant he had not contacted Hadsley about the blackouts.

He finished off the boots as Pilbury pulled on his coat and they walked out into the yard together.

'Get some sleep yourself,' Pilbury said. 'You look nearly as bad as me. Is it warm enough for you in the stables?'

'Yes.'

'Well, you can't stay there all winter. Lodgings will have to be found for you nearby. Although,' his face became pensive, 'I shall miss your company in the evenings.'

'I'll still stay as late as you wish.'

Pilbury's smile returned.

'I'm surrounded by good-hearted souls who seem to think I need looking after.'

'Not at all, sir.'

'Well, goodnight, boy. Sleep well.'

The cloudless night quickly grew cold and Titus shivered beneath the thin blanket. The image of Rancer's face leering at him through his friend's familiar features would not leave his mind. It had been a pleasure to see them twisted with terror at the sound of Samson's voice. Perhaps Rancer had thought his father had returned from the grave.

Titus sat bolt upright.

Throwing off the blanket, he hurried outside. His breath made white billows in the clear air as he hastened across the yard and let himself out of the gate.

# 17

# A BARGAIN

The wall was high. Almost up to the first-storey window.

After a few frustrating minutes scrabbling at its sheer side, he finally managed to swing his leg over then promptly overbalanced and plunged into the flower bed below.

He counted the houses carefully as he scaled each fence and finally stood in the back garden of number nine. Mostly it was wasteland, but there was a small flower bed in the far corner and from it drifted the intoxicating scent of roses.

Beside the kitchen door was a sturdy-looking black drainpipe. Using it for support he jumped onto the kitchen windowsill, then climbed onto the top of the frame and finally the sill of the room on the first floor. It was a precarious position: one foot on the sill, the other toe balanced on a metal seam in the drainpipe that protruded less than an inch. But he was in luck. The sash was open a fraction at the top. He managed to lever it down an inch or so, but it needed a harder push. He took a moment to steady himself, breathing in the cool night air. The curtains were open and, though he couldn't see into the room, he was betting on the fact that Frobisher would have appropriated the front master bedroom for himself.

He was about to give it another go when a hand closed over his. Titus cried out and almost snatched it away.

'Hush! You'll wake my uncle!'

Lilly stood at the window. Lowering the sash she helped him climb into what was evidently her bedroom.

'What's happened?' she whispered. 'Mr Pilbury . . .?'

'He's home safe.'

She lit a candle and pulled the curtains shut. A bed, a stool and a battered trunk were all the furniture in the room. The fire was not lit and the bed had a single thin blanket. The only ornament was a glass jar hanging by wire from a hook on the wall, which contained a single white rose. Lilly sat down on the bed and pulled the fraying hem of her nightdress down over her legs.

'Then what are you doing here?'

She was not angry, just curious.

'I know how to save him,' he said.

Her shadow on the wall behind fluttered in the candlelight.

'But I'll need your help.'

She gazed at him steadily.

'It was Mr Pilbury that made me think of it,' he began. 'He knows there's something up with him. I've never seen him scared of anything or anyone before but he's scared of this. Of going mad. It made me think . . . It made me wonder if there was a way of scaring Rancer. So badly that he leaves Inspector Pilbury for good.'

'Threatening him?'

'No, not that. I did think of it, but he doesn't seem to

fear pain. Did you ever read in the papers about what happened to his father?'

She shook her head, so Titus recounted everything that Stitcher had told him: the tormenting of the boy, the jealousy, the sudden death that might have been murder. Her expression did not alter until he reached the part about the confrontation in the stables.

'. . . And then Sergeant Samson called for me. His voice is deep, very deep, and he was cross with me. I looked over at Rancer and he was terrified.'

The eyes Lilly fixed on him had tiny pinpoints of light deep inside them.

'I think he thought it was his father.'

The room seemed suddenly quieter than ever. Something scrabbled behind the wainscot but neither paid it any attention.

'What if . . .' he continued, his voice barely audible, 'what if you could find him?'

Her lips parted and she drew in breath. Goosebumps ran like cold fingers up his arm.

'Rancer's father?'

Titus nodded. 'In the spirit world.'

They both cried out in alarm as a gust of wind from the open window made the curtain billow in and snuff out the candle. Embarrassed at his cowardice Titus laughed but Lilly did not.

'How long has he been dead?'

'At least fifteen years.'

Lilly swallowed.

'I have never tried to contact a spirit that long passed. He may have already moved on. But he died violently. Or suddenly, at least. And if there was a hint of witchcraft about the death then he may be easier to find. I must ask Florence. I'll do it now.'

She closed her eyes and her breathing became deeper.

Though the room was cold, a bead of sweat formed on Titus's scalp and dribbled down his neck. The curtain billowed, the mouse scrabbled and then she spoke:

'I am here, my dear.'

He recognised the voice from the show at the theatre.

'Florence,' Lilly said, 'I'm with a boy, Titus, a friend.'

Her eyes opened. The normally brown irises swam with a grey mist. Titus shrank from the steady gaze, but he could not look away.

'Hello, Titus,' the old woman said, 'I'm Florence, Lilly's spirit guide.'

Titus managed to nod. The mistiness dispersed as the voice became Lilly's again.

'I need to contact a spirit, long dead. He was murdered by his wife, possibly using witchcraft. His name is Rancer. Father of the one who was hanged.'

The eyes swirled grey again.

'I will speak to them,' Florence said. 'Wait.'

Lilly returned and she and Titus looked at one another in silence. The room now felt very cold and Lilly pulled the blanket out from beneath them and covered their legs.

And then the whispering began. At first it was the merest breath, then it turned into a sigh, then many sighs, until finally it was a susurrating wind that rippled the blanket and ruffled Titus's hair.

Where was it coming from? Was Lilly doing it? But no, her lips were tight shut. Fear crept up his spine. He wanted to spring out of the window and run. She was now blinking rapidly, her hands twisting the blanket into knots. And then her lips moved and it was Florence again.

'He has been found.'

Titus gasped.

'I must advise you, Lilly, do not allow him to speak. There is such malevolence in him, I fear for your safety.'

Lilly swallowed and her voice cracked as she replied.

'Put a proposition to him, then. Tell him his son is now in the spirit world and has taken possession of a friend of ours. We require his help in expelling his spirit. After so many years alone this is a chance to be reunited with his son.'

Silence fell again but Titus could sense the murmurs on the very edge of his hearing.

'Lilly,' it was Florence again, 'he has been long dead, and there is little humanity left in him. Do not try and bargain with him.'

'What did he say?'

'He said nothing.'

'Let him come.'

'No!'

'Let him come through. I'm strong enough.'

For a moment the spirit guide did not respond. Lilly stared straight ahead of her. A vein was pulsing in her neck. Finally Florence spoke again.

'Do not let him overwhelm you, maintain your own consciousness. I will try to restrain him.'

Lilly let go of the blanket and placed her hands in her lap.

'I'm ready,' she said.

Titus glanced out at the clear night sky, and took some

deep breaths to calm himself. There was a sudden yowl from the garden below and then the hissing and snarling of a cat fight. It ended quickly, with a scream of pain from one of the animals. As it died away he heard a sound that made every hair on his body rise up. Rasping breaths, like stone grinding against stone.

For a moment he could not bear to turn back round but when he heard Lilly's querulous but determined voice he felt ashamed of his cowardice.

'Mr Rancer. We wish to ask a service of you.'

The first thing that struck him was the smell. Lilly's breath, as it drifted across to him, had become as foul as a sewer. It was so bad he struggled to turn his face in her direction. She was looking all about her. This time the irises were black but the whites surrounding them had turned scarlet. There was something furtive in the way the eyes flicked this way and that. And then the scarlet tint faded and the eyes were Lilly's once more.

'We know that in life you had great power over your son, Joseph. He feared you and obeyed you in everything.'

The creature gave a guttural chuckle.

'His spirit has taken possession of our friend and we wish him to depart. It is, we believe, in your power to make him do so.'

As Lilly's speech ended Titus watched the tiny capillaries in the medium's eyes dilate with blood. The smell came again in a nauseating wave. For a moment the bloodshot eyes landed on him and his heart stopped, but they slid over him to fix on the rose in the jar. One of Lilly's hands reached up and grasped the flower.

'Will you help us?'

The hand went up to her face and the creature inhaled the flower's perfume.

'Mr Rancer, this is your chance to exact revenge on your son for provoking your murder. Will you help us?'

Suddenly Rancer seemed to become aware that he was not alone. His head jerked this way and that as he tried to find the source of the words. Finally his gaze settled on Titus.

'We can bring you to your son.' Lilly's voice was faltering, exhausted. Her own identity seemed to be struggling to assert itself and the eyes remained those of Rancer's.

The flower fell onto the blanket as those eyes burned into Titus.

'Give him to me,' the voice snarled.

Titus leaped to his feet, knocking over the stool.

'He's yours!' Titus cried. 'If you do as we say.'

The eyes were fixed on Titus and he felt as though spiders were crawling over his skin.

'Very well.'

'Swear. On your soul.'

A laugh like the crackling of burned meat.

'I swear . . . on my sssoul.'

Lilly's right hand reached out and, mesmerised, Titus stepped forward and took it. It was slick with sweat but the strength of it made him draw in breath. Just before his fingers crumpled, the hand went limp and Florence returned.

'Lilly? How are you, my dear?'

'Fine.'

Her voice was weak and in the last few minutes she

seemed to have aged ten years. Titus righted the chair and sat down heavily.

'He chose to depart,' Florence said. 'Next time he may not. You must strengthen yourself if you are to attempt th—'

Before she could finish, the door banged open.

'I knew it!' Frobisher roared. He strode forward and wrenched Lilly from the bed by her arm.

'It's not what you think, Uncle. He's a friend of Inspector Pilbury's . . .'

'Is this how you repay my kindness to you all these years? Grinding with gutter rats under my very nose?'

'I wasn't . . .'

'Let her go,' Titus said, stepping forward.

Frobisher ignored him.

'Filthy whore!' he shouted, then slapped her and pushed her onto the bed so hard her head slammed against the wall. Titus grasped the collar of his nightshirt and pulled the man's hairy face to his.

'She is not a whore,' he said through gritted teeth. 'And I am not a gutter rat.'

Frobisher sneered. Titus let him go but didn't move away from him.

'Uncle,' Lilly said, 'Inspector Pilbury needs my assistance.'

'I told you, NO!'

'But if I can use my gift to aid—'

'Besmirch yourself with the likes of this,' Frobisher interrupted, flinging his arm out at Titus, 'and your gift will leave you, and then where will you be?'

'The gift is MINE to do with as I will,' Lilly cried, rising

194

from the bed. At the crown of her head there was a patch of hair matted with blood.

Frobisher stared at her.

'You need to be taught some respect,' he said finally, his voice low. 'In a moment I'll be back with my belt. If you're still here, boy, you'll get a thrashing too.'

As he turned to go Titus punched him hard in the face. The man's head snapped back, struck the wall, and he fell like a sack of coal onto the floor.

For a minute or two they stood staring at him, waiting for him to come round.

'Is he dead?' Lilly said finally.

Titus bent down and felt his wrist. 'No.' His voice shook a little. He hadn't intended to hurt Frobisher. He looked up at her, worried that he had shocked her, possibly even disgusted her. But she laid a hand on his shoulder and tried to smile. Then her face crumpled.

She bit her lip to try and control it.

'Lilly,' he said, 'you can't ruin your life for this. I'll stay, and when he wakes up I'll explain to him that it was none of your doing.'

He stood up and touched her trembling shoulder.

'I'll find a way without you.'

'How?'

'I don't know yet. But I'm pretty smart, for a gutter rat.'

She looked into his face for a moment, then hurried over to the trunk in the corner. From it she drew a coat, a pair of boots and the pale blue dress, which she began to pull on over her nightdress. Before the lid fell shut Titus caught sight of some drawings that had lain beneath the clothes: ink sketches of faces staring out from deep shadows. The uppermost one was of a young woman in a high-collared black dress. It was disconcertingly lifelike.

'Right,' she said, 'I'm ready.'

'Are you sure? He may not let you return.'

'Better a filthy whore than a slave,' she said, smiling. 'Come, let's go.'

She pulled on the coat.

Titus glanced down at the lumpen shape of Frobisher. He was groaning now. Soon he would wake. Frobisher had asked what Lilly would do without her gift, but without her where would he be? This house, his visits to the club, his smart clothes: all came from her. If she slept the night in the stables with Titus then by the morning Frobisher would be begging her forgiveness.

Big Ben struck midnight as Titus let them through the gate and into the stable courtyard.

'Sorry,' he said, 'it's not exactly comfortable.'

Beatrice and Leopold snored quietly in the shadows and their warm breath had taken the edge off the cold and infused the stable with the sweetness of hay and apples.

He lit a candle and placed in on the upturned half-barrel by his bed.

'You can sleep here.'

'What about you?'

'I'll be fine.'

While she took off her dress he busied himself gathering up hay and piling it into a rough mattress for his own bed. Holding the hay in place with one of the horses' blankets he patted it flat and lay down. By now, Lilly had tucked herself under the blankets of her own bed and was gazing up at the stable roof where the shadows danced in the candlelight.

'Take one of these,' she said, peeling off the upper blanket.

He shook his head.

'We Acre lot don't feel the cold.'

'In that case take my coat. Or I won't sleep for worrying about you.'

He picked it up and pulled it over his shoulders so she couldn't see him shivering. It smelled of lavender.

She rolled over to lie on her side, gathering the blankets under her chin. Her eyes gleamed in the darkness.

'I'm sorry about all this,' he said. 'I should have waited till morning.'

'I'm glad you came. And I like it here. It's just like a home ought to be.'

He chuckled.

'And there was me thinking you weren't mad after all.'

'I feel it sometimes. Sometimes I wish I had my ordinary life again. Just me and Mama. But I suppose I owe it to people to try and help them.'

'You don't owe anyone.'

'It wasn't just that at the start. I thought I'd be helping Mama. Uncle said he'd send most of the money made back to her.'

'But he didn't?'

'She died. Not long after I left.'

'Was that her: the picture in your trunk?'

'No. That's Lady Dora Herschel. She died last year. Her mother asked me to contact her. Francis told me to draw portraits of those I contact to prove to the families that I've really seen them.'

'It's good. At least, it looks like a real person.'

'Yes, it's a good likeness. Though I softened her expression. She did away with herself.'

The silence that followed went on long enough for Titus to think Lilly had gone to sleep. But then she spoke.

'Can I stay here for a few days, to rest and prepare myself?'

'Of course. Though you know Frobisher will come for you.'

'He doesn't know you work here. Just stay out of sight if he comes and he'll have no clue where I've gone.'

She yawned and rolled over to face the wall.

'I must sleep now. It was so draining, trying to hold that creature back.'

She did not move again and her breathing became steady.

He got up and snuffed out the candle, then he bent down and whispered:

'Goodnight, Lilly.'

'Goodnight,' she mumbled.

# 18

# PAYBACK

The next day was warm and bright and the atmosphere in the police station much lighter. Inspector Pilbury took his lunch with the men again and, besides an obsession with checking the kitchen barometer, he seemed healthier and happier. Titus's own mood improved as he began to wonder if the spirit had loosened its grip now that Pilbury was stronger. He visited Lilly regularly, taking her food or drink or the newspaper, but frequently found her lying on the mattress murmuring wordlessly, and would creep out again without interrupting her.

They stayed up late into the evening, even risking sitting out on the step that led into the station. He did not ask who she had been communicating with and she did not say, but she seemed perfectly at ease and became more so as the days wore on.

Frobisher appeared, as they knew he would, blazing about an assault and abduction. He was given short shrift by the duty sergeant, and Lilly and Titus giggled in the darkness of the stables listening to him rail about his lost livelihood and the probable abominations being suffered by his ward at that very moment.

When he left she grew serious.

'He will not be able to afford the mortgage payments without the income from the séances. I'll have to go back or we will lose the house.'

Titus nodded. For a moment they did not move. Leopold kicked at the hay, sending up a cloud of dust motes to drift around them, flashing gold as they spun through the air. Beneath their feet was the almost imperceptible rumble of the underground railway, like a heartbeat. From one of the cells came the mournful singing of a drunk incarcerated earlier for brawling. He was an Irishman and his voice was strong and melodic: he sang a lullaby Titus recognised from his own childhood. She must have known it too because she was smiling and swaying to the rhythm. As she rocked in his direction her shoulder brushed his. She did not move away, but leaned gently into him. A wisp of wind fluttered her hair against his neck. It smelled of hay. Her white hand lay still in her lap, palm upwards as if waiting to be touched.

Then Samson started bellowing for the horses.

The following Friday it was with a light heart that Titus turned his steps towards Little Almonry. Though still sullen, Hannah looked healthy enough, and when he told her he was to be paid in a week's time and so would be back to collect her, she could not keep the sparkle from her eyes. When she asked after the Inspector he told her that he was back to his normal self. There was no sense in worrying her.

As he watched them all troop back in for supper he noticed that her hair was finally beginning to grow again, and now curled about her head like a halo. The image made him smile. There were few children less angelic.

Leaving via the porter's office he told the man that Hannah would be leaving soon, and thanked him for all their kindness to her. To his surprise the porter actually reached out and shook his hand.

'I like to see a family pick itself up again,' he said. 'It does not happen often enough.'

On the way back to the station he found himself humming a music hall tune and, as if to confirm that the fates had finally decided to smile on him, he discovered a shining new penny in the gutter. Victoria's face, absurdly young and pretty, had the whisper of a smile.

*Oh, my love is like a red, red rose that's newly sprung in June . . .*

He passed the Horse and Groom. The some father and son were there, and the boy called after him, 'Got any errands, sir?'

Titus grinned at the title but shook his head and walked on.

*My love is like a melody that's sweetly played in tune . . .*

He took a detour via the river and watched the barges bumping and crowding at the opposite wharf, the men scolding and teasing one another. London held a million opportunities for an enterprising and bright young man. He liked the idea of life as a dredgerman, unfettered by the rules and constraints on land.

*As fair as you are, my lovely lass, so deep in love am I . . .*

For a moment he was tempted to toss the coin out across the water and wish on it, but he managed to restrain himself and instead gave a little prayer of thanks to whichever god might be listening.

*And I will love you still, my dear, till all the seas go dry . . .*

He noticed that one of the bargemen in the nearest skiff was not much older than he himself. He was joking around with an older man in a nearby boat.

*Till all the seas go dry, my dear, and the rocks melt with the sun . . .*

And then suddenly the older man leaped from his own boat, into the boy's. It pitched and rolled and there were cries of alarm from the other boatmen. The man hurled himself at the boy and Titus realised they hadn't been joking at all. He tried to make out what was happening but the two bodies fell into the boat in a writhing mass. A light mist was creeping over the water, and a moment later it had engulfed boats and men. The voices became indistinct, but still conveyed their warning or threat, like the calls of animals. Then one of the voices rose above the others, in a bellow that reverberated across the river.

'I'll pay you back for that!'

The phrase was familiar and for the rest of the way back to the station Titus tried to place where he had heard it recently. Getting back took longer than he thought as the mist deepened, and when he finally approached the gates it was past six o'clock. The air was now thick and yellow and he could hear the coughs of men out in the yard. Alone in the dark stables Lilly would be cold and hungry. He shouldn't have dawdled so long.

A shadow loomed up as he let himself in.

'Inspector Pilbury? Is that you? We've been worried, sir. On a night like this you shouldn't go out alone . . .'

Samson's voice tailed off as he drew close enough to make out Titus's features.

'It's not him,' he called back over his shoulder, then melted away.

'D'you think one of us should go after him?' a disembodied voice said.

'Which way did he go?'

'Bill saw him. Where was it, Bill?'

'Up towards Little Almonry, I think . . .'

The voices ricocheted around Titus as he stood alone in the smog, and suddenly he knew where he had heard the phrase before. *You'll pay me back.*

Titus had stolen a child from Rancer, so he would pay the debt with another.

Hannah.

## 19

# HELL

'Lilly! Where are you?'

The tendrils of smog had even penetrated the stable: the horses were spectres in the gloom, Lilly's empty bed a slab of darkness in the corner.

Titus ran back outside and across the courtyard to the kitchen. Had she sneaked in to warm herself by the fire while the officers hunted for Pilbury?

The kitchen was deserted. He snatched up a paper and pen and scrawled a note:

*He means to kill Hannah.*
*I am going to find him.*

He left the note on Lilly's bed then ran out of the gate, left open in the confusion.

'Lilly!' he cried. 'Lilly!'

A shape loomed out of the darkness.

'Lilly! Thank God! He means to kill Hannah!'

But the shape resolved itself into something twisted and cadaverous.

'You lied to me,' the figure rasped, lurching forward.

'You said you'd come and find me and you never did. I'm gonna kill you now.'

'Stitcher? My God . . .'

But the boy drew no weapon. Instead he grasped Titus around the throat and drove him backwards against the courtyard wall, so hard that the gate thrummed. As Titus clawed at the hands around his neck he could feel every contour of Stitcher's bones. The skin stretched over them was flaking off. His hair was falling out in patches. His clothes were rags.

Grief had killed all the humanity in him, leaving only rage and hatred. The only living things left of him were his eyes which burned with enough passion and loathing to keep a thousand corpses on their feet. He opened his mouth and a stench of decay struck Titus full in the face. But he did not speak: his mouth opened wider to reveal blackened teeth embedded in brown and swollen gums. Stitcher meant to tear him apart with his very teeth.

With a final burst of effort Titus managed to loosen the hands long enough to cry out, 'Charly's murderer! I know where he is!'

The horrible mouth closed. The eyes narrowed.

'Another lie . . .' he hissed.

'He's going after Hannah. Please, Stitch, let me go. I need to stop him.'

Stitcher stared at him a moment then the skeletal hands loosened.

'He'll take her to the river,' Stitcher said.

And then suddenly the hands were snatched away and Titus collapsed to the ground. Stitcher was gone, swallowed by the fog.

Titus hauled himself upright, waited until the black spots had cleared from his vision, then set off at a run.

He arrived outside the workhouse gate just as they were locking it. Taking one glance at the pinched and sour faces of the officials he did not bother to request entry, just kicked the gate open with all his might, sending them sprawling, then sprinted across the yard to the porter's door.

The porter was writing in a ledger and looked up in surprise as Titus burst in.

'Bring me my sister!' he bellowed.

'How dare you! Get out of here this minute!'

'Bring her now,' Titus repeated, snatching up a letter opener from the desk and thrusting it towards the man's quivering belly, 'or I'll skewer you like a hog roast.'

'She is not here . . .' the porter stammered, his face growing a lighter shade of puce.

'Is she asleep? Go and wake her!'

'The policeman came for her.'

Titus blanched. He had told Hannah himself that Pilbury was much recovered.

'When?'

'No more than ten minutes since . . .'

He flew out of the door and back into the thick air.

But his mind, stricken with panic, simply could not organise the street names into their familiar pattern and he blundered about, doubling back on himself, going round in circles.

Eventually he found his way to the Acre, but he'd been away too long, and the wicked tangle of streets punished him for it. Soon he was utterly lost, and blind in the fog. Stretching out his arms he took a few steps forward until he found the wall of a building. He stood with his back to it and peered into the grey. Someone was coming towards him. Stitcher? He shrank back and lifted a protective arm to his face, but the figure dissolved into swirling eddies. The air was filled with phantoms.

He heard a whispering, very close by, and fear twisted his guts. The voices were all around him, to the left, to the right, beneath him.

Then he let out a sharp laugh of relief.

He was standing over the gutter. Oozing along beneath him was a babbling stream of human sewage. And there was only one direction it would be heading.

He followed the gutter until it went underground – this meant he must be near civilisation for the well-to-do did not wish to see the passage of their own filth. Sure enough he rounded the next corner and came out into Victoria Street. Unable to see the edge of the pavement he blundered straight into the path of a carriage but it was barely moving thanks to the smog. The thoroughfare was as silent as the grave, and all he could hear was the rush of his own blood in his ears. Several agonising minutes later, his hands found the Broad Sanctuary street sign. Now he could smell the river. He set off at a run, rebounding off lamp posts and letter boxes, in the direction of the bridge.

His eyes streamed in the cold and murky air, and his eyeballs ached with the strain of staring into the fog. He could make out nothing, not the soaring Abbey, the Houses of Parliament, nor even Big Ben.

Surely, with a head start of just ten minutes, even given

the time he had been lost, they could not have got here before him. He'd run all the way, and his heart was banging hard enough to blur his vision. He did not care if it gave out on him afterwards but it must keep working until he found them. And, if it came to that, until he killed Pilbury. He realised that in his hurry he had forgotten both the truncheon and the knife. He would have no means of attack or defence, apart from whatever stones or pieces of metal he might pick up on the beach. He hurried across what he thought must be St Margaret Street and onto the bridge, then got down onto his knees and crawled about until he found a loose brick at the edge of the pavement.

Now he could hear the swish of the river. He was close. Voices in the fog.

Perhaps it was just the murmur of the river. No, they were coming from the other side of the bridge. He willed his blood to stop rushing long enough for him to listen. They were close now, almost parallel, one deep, one high-pitched. His blood did stop then, and he heard his sister's voice quite clearly.

'So he is to be *Constable* Titus Adams!'

She giggled. The deeper voice murmured.

'What, down here?'

Titus bounded across the road and did not stop until he slammed into the wall on the other side.

'What the hell was that?' Hannah squeaked. 'It's blooming creepy this fog!'

'Hannah!'

He blundered in the direction of her voice.

And there she was. At the top of the steps. Her hair a

mass of curls, like a crown of gold thorns. There was no-one with her. Had he already gone down? In that case they were safe.

'Hannah!'

'Jesus and Mary!' she yelled, clutching her chest. 'I thought you was a murderer!'

He ran up and pulled her into his arms.

She shook herself free, then leaned over the stairs that led down into the fog.

'It's Titus!' she called down. 'He was not too busy to come, after all!'

Then, before he could stop her, she hopped onto the first step. Her foot and ankle were swallowed by swirling white.

'Come down, Titus. Mr Pilbury says there is a tall ship coming by any moment, on its way to the Indies!'

Titus grasped her arm.

'It's a lie! The ships can't come so far up.'

She stared at him in confusion and then gave a little gasp and stared down into the fog.

'I'm all right, Mr Pilbury, I won't slip. You can let go of me leg.'

'Shake him off,' Titus said urgently, grasping her arm.

'But you said he was better . . .'

'Kick him off, Hannah!'

But she could not. She whimpered as a yank from below almost made her slip. Beneath them, the fog lapped at her bare leg.

'Help me!' she whimpered.

Titus hurled the brick down into the fog but a moment later it thudded harmlessly on the sand and the grip on

Hannah's leg did not loosen. He thrust his arms under her, and wrenched with all his might. She screamed and a bone-white hand jerked into view, clamped around her ankle.

'Rancer, let her go!' Titus shouted.

'Rancer? Who's Rancer?' she shrieked.

The sinews of the hand flexed and then Hannah plunged downwards. As she slipped through Titus's grasp he managed to catch hold of her hand before every other part of her was drowned in fog.

Her wrist twisted this way and that as her body flailed.

He heaved until stars exploded before his eyes while she screamed and screamed, but Rancer did not release her. Titus paused to catch his breath and steel himself for another attempt and at that moment he saw another presence closing in through the fog.

Was this the accomplice; the one that had returned the whistle outside St Mary Rouncivall? The fog turned blue, as if it was dissipating to reveal a clear sky. Then the blue resolved itself into a woman's dress.

'Lilly!'

'Am I in time? I went to see Francis . . .'

'Pull off my boot . . .!'

'What?'

'Pull it off!'

He flung out his foot and she dropped down beside him. It took an eternity of fumbling with the laces before finally the huge, heavy thing thudded onto the pavement and lay on its side, the rows of hobnails gleaming along its sole.

'Give me the boot, and take Hannah's other arm,' he said urgently. 'That's it . . . Now, pull as hard as you can!'

Titus braced his leg against the bridge wall. His arm

shuddered. Lilly groaned with the effort and Hannah shrieked. Then the shrieks became more piercing and her head and shoulders emerged from the fog. This was what he was waiting for, to ensure he did not harm her. He hurled the boot as hard as he could directly down into the swirling grey. There was a thud, a cry of pain, and then they were pulling against nothing. Hannah burst out of the fog and sent them tumbling in a heap on the pavement.

'Get her away!' Titus hissed. 'I'll wait for him.'

'He'll kill you!' Lilly said, already pulling Hannah away from the staircase.

'He'll try. You must act quickly.'

She nodded and vanished.

Titus sat with his back to the wall. The wind was picking up and his hair whispered against the brickwork. The shadowy column of Big Ben was becoming darker and more distinct every moment. Soon the smog would be gone. Rancer would know his plans had been thwarted. Would the man that ascended the steps from the beach be just a confused and terrified Pilbury? If so their own plan was in tatters. Titus would have to tell Hadsley or Samson. Pilbury would go to the gallows or the asylum.

A noise to his right, coming from the flight of steps. Scraping. A moan.

He drew in his knees and held his breath.

The scrape of grit against stone. Heavy breathing.

Fingers crept around the wall, inches from his feet. Then a man's torso rose from the mist. He climbed onto the pavement and crawled forward on all fours, blood drooling from his nose and mouth, panting like an animal.

Rancer's presence seemed to have pushed its own features into Pilbury's: the nose looked more bulbous, the jaw sharper and more brutal. Titus could see the reflection of black eyes in the pooling blood on the stones. Now he knew for certain. This was not Pilbury. The eyes met his and slowly the head turned.

He was leaning heavily on his arms and it would take a moment for him to adjust his centre of gravity. Titus's hand darted forward and snatched the handcuffs from Rancer's coat pocket. Rancer hesitated, his attention caught by the glittering metal. It was enough. The cuff was around his wrist and Titus snapped the bar across. Now that Rancer understood what was happening he tore himself away, jerking the free cuff out of Titus's reach. Titus sprang at him and they rolled onto the pavement, Titus ending up underneath. The weight on top of him was crushing, squeezing the air from his lungs. Rancer's cuffed hand was by Titus's head. Titus could feel the cold metal against his ear. This might be his only chance. Raising his arm he found the open shackle and thrust his own wrist inside then snapped the bar closed. For a moment both of them were still, then Rancer roared in fury, and started bucking and yanking to free himself. Somehow, Titus managed to turn the key in the lock, slide it out and toss it across the street.

'So, you think you can hold me?' Rancer bellowed. 'I'll tear off your arm!'

'Get off him, beast!'

The voice was Hannah's. She kicked Rancer in the head and now the weight lifted off Titus as Rancer staggered to his feet. Titus was dragged along the pavement by the handcuff.

'*Hail, spirits of the . . . sacred . . . river,*' Rancer grunted. Titus's knees scraped against the ground.

'Stay back or I'll skewer you!' Hannah screeched.

From the folds of her dress she drew out a spoon, the end of which had been filed to a point.

Rancer reached forward and grasped her by the arm, driving his thumb into the tendons of her elbow. With a squeal of pain she dropped the weapon into the gutter. With his other hand he grasped Titus's hair.

'Two gifts. The gods will bless you tonight, Mother.'

He turned and dragged them both towards the staircase.

'*From one who has passed beyond the realm . . .*'

The chuckle began so low it was just the rumble of distant thunder. Hannah was shouting too much to hear, but Titus caught the new sound immediately. As the mist darkened and he began to make out Lilly's shape the chuckle took on a shrill edge of glee. Her face swam out of the fog. Her mouth was twisted into a smile but her eyes were dead, and the voice that came from her pale lips was the same harsh rasp that had so chilled him that night in her bedroom.

'*Ah, my boy. How I have missed you.*'

It was no more than a whisper, but Rancer froze.

'Come, embrace me.'

Titus threw himself backwards, catching Rancer off balance. Hannah must have sensed the opportunity for she pushed forward and the big man pivoted and swung round.

'*You shall have an apple,*' Lilly sang. '*You shall have a plum. You shall have a rattle, when your daddy comes . . .*'

Where his leg pressed against Rancer's, Titus felt a sudden warmth. Rancer had wet himself.

Lilly raised her arms and the fingers hung, dead and grey, like the innards of a crab.

'Come. You are no stranger to a corpse's arms.'

'MOTHER!' Rancer howled.

His voice echoed out across the river. Now that the fog had dispersed Titus could see it slithering all the way down from Tower Bridge. A black, hungry eel.

'The witch still lives?' Lilly said. 'I see she has taught you her trade. Child killer.'

'She made me do it,' Rancer whispered. 'They were gifts to the river gods, to prolong her life.'

Lilly took a step forward.

'Then we shall await her together.'

Rancer whimpered, then jerked Titus forward as he tried to clasp his hands in prayer.

'*Our Father who art in Heaven,*' he began. '*Hallowed be thy . . .*'

'Pray to the devil. He is your master.'

Titus hissed into Rancer's ear, 'Leave Pilbury, now! Before it is too late!'

But Rancer could not hear him. His eyes were on stalks. His skin grey and glistening.

'*Thy kingdom come,*' he muttered. '*Thy will be done . . .*'

Hannah twisted away and was free.

'*Dance to your daddy, my little laddy . . .*' Lilly sang in that dreadful rasp.

As she came closer her breath was rank with the same stench that had filled the room in Fulham.

'Kiss me, Joey.'

Rancer moaned. Titus braced himself to hold him, though the man seemed too weak with terror to think of escape.

Lilly's hands closed around Pilbury's face, then she bent into him. Her lips parted.

Rancer's free hand flew up to his face and tore at the iron grip on his cheek. His chest shuddered as he tried to scream, but the sound was muffled. Lilly drank it down.

The blue dress was drenched in sweat. Cords of bulbous veins snaked across every part of her exposed skin, throbbing rapidly. It suddenly occurred to Titus that she might not survive this ordeal and his heart clenched.

Her face pressed in, pushing Rancer's jaw wider and wider.

Far away, in some lost country, Titus heard Hannah crying.

Pilbury's body suddenly convulsed and Lilly's head snapped backwards.

Then Titus was falling, a great weight on top of him. His forehead struck the pavement and the weight pinned him. Had Rancer broken free? If so they were all doomed. Rancer would overpower him and Hannah and finish what he came here to do. Then he would kill and kill until he was found out and Pilbury was hanged.

He managed to heave himself out from beneath Rancer's body.

But it was not Rancer's body.

Inspector Pilbury lay on his back, taking great gasps of air.

'Sir?' Titus croaked. 'Mr Pilbury?'

Pilbury's head rolled sideways and he gazed at Titus.

The river stink had gone from his breath, to be replaced with the sweet familiar fragrance of whisky.

'Titus?'

'Yes, sir?'

'What . . . is . . . happening?'

But before Titus could formulate a reply, Pilbury's eyes rolled back into his head and he fainted.

Hannah skidded to her knees next to Titus. She produced the key to the handcuffs and expertly unsnicked them. Removing the cuff from his wrist she was about to fasten it on Pilbury's when Titus stopped her hand. She looked at him as if he had gone mad.

'I'll explain later. Please, trust me.'

And, for once, his sister did as she was told.

The policeman breathed deeply and peacefully as the colour seeped back into his face like a sunrise.

The two children got up. And then Titus remembered Lilly.

She lay on the pavement, seemingly motionless, but when Titus ran over he saw that her face was alive with shadows and shapes. One minute she would open her clear dark eyes and attempt to speak, the next they would become grey and glassy.

'Lilly! Say something!'

For a moment she looked up at him and seemed to know him, but then her eyes focused on something he could not see.

'Depart,' she said quietly in her own voice. 'We are done.'

The whites of her eyes reddened and her bloodless lips bent into a smile.

'Farewell.' The voice was like dead leaves blowing away.

For a moment her whole body was tugged upwards, as if a line were attached to the bodice of her dress, and Titus thought she might actually rise into the air. But then she slumped back and her eyes opened, clear and brown. She smiled.

'He's gone.'

Her smile faded as she saw Pilbury's body at the top of the stairs and she struggled to get up.

'Is he dead?'

'Only fainted, I think.'

She hurried over and bent her face to Pilbury's.

'He's breathing!' She turned back to them. 'We must decide what to say when he wakes. When he finds out what he has done . . .'

'He must never find out!' Titus said urgently. 'It would kill him. He'd feel like he had to confess to them, and then he'd go to the gallows and it would all have been for nothing. Besides, it wasn't him that did the murders – we know that – those that did the killing have been punished for it. He was just as innocent as the children.'

'What are you talking about?' Hannah said from a little distance away, but when Titus beckoned her over she wouldn't come nearer.

'It wasn't Mr Pilbury that grabbed you . . .' he called quietly across to her.

'Yes it was, I saw his face.'

'No. It was someone else. Someone evil who had got inside him. I'll explain properly later but for now just keep your mouth shut and go along with everything we say, all right?'

217

Hannah hesitated, then nodded.

'We can say it was the old woman,' Lilly said. 'That she'd faked being sick all along.'

'Yeah,' Titus said, 'he can't remember half of it anyway and . . .'

He glanced up at Lilly's face and his voice died. The flush had drained from her cheek and she was staring over his shoulder with an expression of utter horror.

'Lilly? What is it? Is he back?' he said, but she did not reply.

He followed her gaze.

Something was coming towards them, from the direction of the Acre. A strange, creeping thing. From it came whining, choking sounds that might have been speech.

'Florence?' Lilly whispered. 'Do you hear?'

But Florence did not come.

The shape resolved itself into a person, slithering on its belly like a snake. Its head was bent but its arms worked furiously, the fingers clawing the ground and dragging the body forward.

Lilly stood and backed away until she came up sharply against the wall.

The figure crawled off the pavement on the other side of the bridge but tumbled forward in the process and landed on its back. The old woman was even more cadaverous than when Titus had last seen her. Every bump and ridge of her skull stood out painfully, every knobble of bone at her elbows and wrists. The tumour had grown so huge that it forced her head over to touch her shoulder. Righting herself with a grunt she continued crawling towards them.

'Titus,' Hannah wailed, 'what is it?'

But Titus's attention was on Lilly, frozen against the wall. Her irises rolled back into her head.

Mrs Rancer was now halfway across the road and Titus could make out some words.

'Come, Hecate. Astarte. Baal. Mab. Rise, Judas, and engulf her. Lilith. Balor. Taranis. Nemain. Devour her . . .'

The list of names continued. He recognised only one. The slayer of Christ.

'What's she saying?' Hannah said, tugging at his arm, her eyes out on stalks.

'She is summoning monsters,' Titus said. 'To destroy Lilly's mind. Give me your spoon.'

He held out his hand but she shook her head.

'I dropped it!'

The old woman was almost upon them. Thrusting Hannah back behind him he launched himself at her, flinging himself on top of her, and the two rolled over into the gutter. Her curses were replaced by furious screams. Old lady or not, he struck her twice around the face and she finally fell silent.

He scrambled over to Lilly. The dreadful sightless eyes fluttered closed and she slumped to the ground, breathing heavily. He knelt beside her, speaking urgently, slapping her on the cheek. Her breathing began to ease.

Behind him, Hannah was crying.

'It's all right,' he murmured. 'The spirits are gone. We're safe.'

'No, we're not,' Hannah shrieked. 'Titus!'

He spun round. The old woman was rearing up behind him like a cobra. As he sprang to his feet she raised Hannah's sharpened spoon and plunged it into his thigh.

Hannah screamed.

He staggered backwards and came up against the balustrade of the bridge. The blade had gone into the tender flesh that was just healing after the stable boy's attack, but this cut was far, far deeper. His blood drew an arc across the pale stone.

Triumph gave the old lady some kind of terrible strength because somehow she managed to heave herself upright, grinning at him from that sideways head. Now she grasped Hannah by the hair and began dragging her towards the staircase.

But at that moment something struck her from behind, sending her hurtling against the balustrade. Her bones crunched and there was an audible pop, as if something inside her had burst. Hannah tore herself away as a creature of nightmares took the old woman in its claws. The face that snarled into Mrs Rancer's was no longer human.

'Stitcher?' Hannah whispered in disbelief, but the remnants of the boy did not hear her.

He flung his head back and howled up at the blade of moon.

'CHARLYYYYYYYYYY!'

The scream died away and Stitcher lowered his head. Titus could not see his expression, only the awful horror of the old woman as she stared into his face. Her lips moved silently. Blood and yellow mucus seeped from the corner of her mouth.

'Shall we go?' Stitcher hissed.

The old woman's lips pursed. 'W . . . w . . . w . . .'

'Where?' he said, and for a moment it was the old Stitcher's voice: amused, arrogant, teasing.

220

'The place where I have been since you took my brother.'

He lifted her into an embrace.

And with that he leaped over the balustrade. Her howl of despair was cut short by a splash, and then there was silence.

Titus staggered forward, the blood still pumping from his thigh. Leaning heavily on the balustrade he hauled himself along to the flight of steps then stumbled down them, his bare foot sliding on the algae.

'Stitcher!' he cried hoarsely as he lurched down the beach. At the river's edge he swayed a little, scanning the black water around him. But there was not enough substance left in those two creatures even for the merest ripple. The icy mud oozed up between his bare toes. Bending low to the surface of the water he spread his arms wide and made sweep after sweep of the foreshore, going deeper and deeper until he was moving on tiptoes and the stinking waves lapped his face, red with his own blood.

Hannah's voice drifted to him from the shore.

'Come back! They're gone.'

Suddenly he felt more tired than he had ever felt in his life. The current lifted his legs and laid him out on the waves, as if they were a bed of feathers. His eyelids were heavy as the pile of damp linen in the corner. He tried to remember if he had done the stitching of Mr Tarrant's hat or read Hannah's bedtime story. It would have to wait now. He was so tired and the light was failing. The blanket billowed gently over his face.

Then something tore it off and he was wrenched up out of the warm embrace of the water and into the biting air.

'No!' he cried, but the arms that imprisoned him did not loosen.

'Stay awake, Titus,' Pilbury's voice said. 'Don't leave us now, lad.'

His head lolled backwards as Pilbury carried him out of the water. The pain had gone but he was so desperately tired. If he might only close his eyes for just a few seconds . . .

But a moment later he was slammed down on the beach.

He blinked and opened his eyes. Lights burst at the corners of his vision, like exploding stars.

'Stay awake, Titus,' Pilbury said sternly, kneeling over him. 'Hannah has gone for the doctor. Can you hear me, boy? Answer me!'

'Yes,' he mumbled.

'I'm going to try and stem the blood loss. It may hurt.'

Titus watched lazily as the Inspector stripped off his jacket and unclipped his braces. His right leg had gone numb and he felt nothing as the leather strap was wound around his thigh. Then Pilbury braced himself and pulled. Titus screamed and writhed as pain tore through him, but Pilbury held him down with both hands, pressing his shoulders into the hard pebbles.

'Stay still! You will only weaken yourself further.'

Titus rolled his eyes to the sky and the darkness closed in.

When he came round again Lilly was bending over him, her face as white as the moon.

'. . . There! He has woken again!' she cried.

'Where is Hadsley?' Pilbury cried. He was standing a little way off, shirtless, holding aloft a flaming piece of wood.

'Over here!' he bellowed up at the bridge. 'Hadsley!'

Lilly too was scouring the bridge. Titus raised his hand and turned her face to his. His arm felt heavy as lead and he had to let it drop.

'Look after Hannah,' he murmured.

Lilly struck away the tears from her cheeks and grasped his shirt in her fist.

'Don't you dare!' she said. 'You stay here!'

He smiled as the shafts of moonlight that fell around her shifted and melted together until they seemed to be figures of light, gathering on all sides of him. Her hot tears splashed on his face. She was darkening, while the moonlight figures were getting brighter.

He let his eyelids start to sink.

'No!'

The arms were snatched away and he heard quick little footsteps receding down the pebbles. He managed to force his eyes to open and he saw that she had begun to wade out into the river. When the water was up to her waist she stopped and tipped her head back.

'Spirits, hear me!'

A light wind whipped up the water and snatched at her hair. The moonlight on the wave tips was so bright it hurt him to look at them.

'Too long I have troubled you. Torn you from your peace. Delayed your passage to the blessed realm.'

She raised her arms and held them clasped above her, as if in prayer, and as she did so the wind grew stronger, blowing clouds across the moon, blotting out the light.

The darkness was kind, the wind stroked his cheek, the beach seemed to undulate beneath him, rocking him like a cradle. Only his heart banged and banged, like a drum in his ear.

'I have been a burden to you who wish to leave the cares of this world behind.'

The wind was now strong enough to blow wet grit into his face but he did not have the strength to close his lips. There were other voices now – two men and a shrill child's voice: Hannah's.

Bang, bang went his heart, but slower now.

The world slewed. The dull colours of water and sky smeared. His body was entirely numb. Still, in the distance Lilly's voice went on.

'I swear I will leave you in peace, forever, if you will do one thing for me.'

The wind howled around him as if it wished to pick him up and carry him off. He closed his eyes and let his mind drift. The sound of Lilly's voice receded to a murmur. His heart finally quietened: a thud, then a scrape.

'Do not take him with you. Let him stay!'

Peace washed over him. His heart gave a flutter, then another frailer one. He was just a single tiny point of consciousness in a universe of blackness. And then that point blinked out.

His heart whispered in the darkness.

His heart stopped.

. . .

. .

.

And then his heart gave a single beat.

It fluttered, then thudded, then banged.

The point of consciousness rapidly expanded. His thoughts hurtled into focus and his eyes snapped open.

Lilly stood in the river, facing him.

She opened her mouth, but before she could speak pain crashed on top of him with the force of a speeding train. His head hammered, his lungs burned. His thigh was a huge throbbing, searing mass of agony that made him rear up and tear at the bindings. He took a huge gasp of air and screamed.

They came over to him and he felt arms fighting him and voices barking at him and women sobbing and through it all a man laughing and crying: 'It's a miracle, it's a miracle!'

# 20

# A NEW HOME

He woke in a room with roses on the wall. The curtains were drawn but a fine line of brilliance between them suggested it was broad daylight outside. He wondered how long he had been asleep.

Being careful not to move too quickly and worsen the dull ache around his temples Titus shuffled up on the pillows. His thigh throbbed but the pain was bearable and he could move his toes and stretch the muscles of his calf.

He thought he recognised the room but couldn't quite believe it. He needed more light to be certain.

Pulling back the covers he slid his injured leg to the · floor and gingerly put some weight on it. It throbbed a little more. Sliding the other leg down he stood up and swayed for a moment as the blood rushed from his head. He was wearing a pair of striped pyjama trousers and a white vest that was slightly too large for him.

Taking a step forward on his good leg he leaned against the solid black chest of drawers below the window and opened the curtains.

Sure enough, the room looked out over a garden. A young woman and a girl sat at a little table by a pond: the woman was drawing the girl. He watched them until his injured leg began to ache, then he turned and went back to the bed. A glass of water stood on the bedside table and he realised he was parched with thirst.

As he was drinking, the memories flooded back to him. Replacing the glass he sank back onto the pillow and closed his eyes.

A voice spoke from the doorway.

'The wanderer returns.'

He made to get up again.

'No, lie back,' Pilbury said, coming over. 'You don't know how close you came to . . . Well. How are you feeling?'

The Inspector sat down on a stool by the bed. His face was pink with pleasure and, instead of his usual musk of whisky, he smelled faintly of soap.

'Did they find Stitcher?' Titus said.

The Inspector's smile faded. 'They pulled him out of the river a few miles down from the bridge. The old woman washed up nearby. There will be time to grieve for him, but for now let us think of happier things. How are you feeling?'

Titus closed his eyes for a moment and into his head came an image of Stitcher and Charly sitting on the wall outside their house: Stitcher holding up a gold pocket watch to spin in the sunlight, and Charly trying to catch the light that danced across his legs.

'Titus?'

He opened his eyes. 'I'm fine,' he said. 'Much better. I can be back at work tomorrow if they will give me a crutch.'

'Tomorrow's Sunday. And, besides, our stable boy is back to prime physical fitness, more's the pity.'

Titus's heart sank.

'Your sister will be delighted to see you back with us again but before I fetch her, there's something I would very much like to discuss with you.'

Pilbury looked down at his hands for a moment, turning them over and gazing at the lines that criss-crossed the palms.

'The night of your injury,' he said finally, 'I can remember nothing of it.'

He looked up and searched Titus's face. Titus kept his own expression neutral.

'Lilly told me it was the woman, Mrs Rancer. And that she was drowned by the brother of one of the victims.'

He rubbed his face with a hand that trembled a little.

'I will not ask you again, I swear. First thing tomorrow I will get Hadsley to examine me. But please, Titus, tell me what happened.'

So Titus told him.

He told him that Lilly had summoned the latest victim who confirmed Pilbury's suspicions that Mrs Rancer was continuing where her son left off. The old woman's sickness had been faked all along, Titus assured him: she was not the weak, dying thing they had all thought but hale and hearty as her son. He described how he and the Inspector had used Hannah as bait and then followed the two of them to the river, where Pilbury had arrested the old woman in the act. She admitted everything, claiming that the murders were sacrifices to the river gods to prolong her life, but before they could take her back to the station Stitcher appeared and seized the old lady, leaping from the bridge to drown them both.

Pilbury accepted it all, frowning and nodding slowly throughout, as if trying to recall his own part in the proceedings. Afterwards, aside from the birdsong in the trees outside the window, all was quiet for some time.

'Why was Lilly at the river?' Pilbury asked eventually.

'We asked her to come and tend to Hannah afterwards.'

'It was madness to risk Hannah's safety like that,' Pilbury muttered. 'What was I thinking?'

He slumped against the wall, gazing into the fireplace, his expression troubled.

'You seem a lot better, sir,' Titus ventured. 'Perhaps your distractedness was simply absorption in the case.'

'Perhaps,' Pilbury said, then gave a weak smile. 'And I have been drinking far too much whisky.'

Before he could say more, there was a cry from the doorway and a moment later something powerful struck Titus in the chest. For a moment he could not breathe and his ribs felt as if they were about to crumple.

'Hannah!' Pilbury cried. 'Be careful!'

The weight was lifted and Hannah stood beside the bed smiling almost shyly.

Their eyes locked for a moment.

'Lilly told me everything what happened,' she said clearly, 'and I don't mind a bit.'

So she had been hoodwinked too. This was probably a good thing. It was questionable whether she could be trusted with the truth.

But then she winked at him. Titus's eyes widened, then he smiled.

'Good girl,' he murmured.

229

He pulled himself up to a sitting position. He wouldn't let Hannah see him weakened. She'd only take advantage.

'And tomorrow we move back to our new home in the Acre.'

Hannah shot a look at Inspector Pilbury.

'Yes,' he said, 'Hannah told me that you were saving money for a cellar room in Old Pye Street.'

'That's right. If you don't mind giving me my wages then . . .'

'Titus. Those cellars are uninhabitable.'

Titus stared at him.

'The Tyburn runs beneath the Acre, and not very deep beneath. After heavy rain the cesspools flood and sewage bubbles up into the basements. You'd be dead from cholera by the spring.'

Titus blinked. His mouth had gone very dry. He could feel Hannah watching him, waiting for him to speak, waiting for him to explain how they would avert this new disaster.

'Well, you see, Titus,' Pilbury went on, drawing his pipe from his pocket, 'I have been thinking about this whole situation.'

He pulled out the tobacco and began loading the bowl. Its moist fragrance drifted across to Titus, smelling unbearably of home and warmth.

'I don't suppose I ever told you, but I had a daughter once.' He tamped down the tobacco. 'She would be Hannah's age now.'

Hannah stared at him in astonishment.

'Yes,' he said to her, 'the room you are sleeping in was hers.'

Titus sensed where this might be going and his heart leapt at the same moment his throat tightened. They would be separated, but she would live the life he had always dreamed she would.

'Do you like it?'

Hannah nodded.

'My housekeeper, Mrs Membery,' he went on, 'makes the best fruitcakes in the whole of London, and when I am at work she could be home to play games and bake cakes and plait hair. Would you like to stay, Hannah, and keep an old man company?'

A smile crept over her face, but then it clouded. She shook her head.

'Hannah!' Titus cried. 'Of course you will!'

She looked away from the policeman and laced her fingers into Titus's.

Titus flushed with shame and despair and love and apologised so profusely it took him some time to realise that Pilbury was laughing.

'Did you think I would abandon your brother to sleep in a ditch?' he said.

Hannah nodded and wiped a tear from the corner of her eye.

'Nonsense!' His laughter subsided. He cleared his throat once or twice and when he spoke again, his voice was rather gruff. 'I should be honoured if the two of you would stay here and live with me.'

His eyes met Titus's and held his gaze for just a moment before glancing away.

Titus could not speak. His ribs strained at the pressure in his chest.

'Right, well,' Pilbury sprang up and strode to the door, 'lots to do. Talk it out between the two of you and let me know what you decide.'

The last part of the sentence sailed back to them as he hurried away down the corridor.

Titus lay back on the plump pillow and, as he did so, he felt all the shame and despair and loss and grief of the last few years wash away from him, like an ebb tide drawing away the filth and detritus from the shore and carrying it out to sea.

Then Hannah punched him hard on the shoulder.

'You are gonna say yes?'

He kept his face grave for a moment, then, when her eyes were round and her lip had begun to tremble, he smiled at her.

'You bloody sod,' she mumbled, swiping the tears away with her fists.

He pushed back the blankets and gingerly stood up.

'Come on, we'll go and find him.'

As he made his way to the door he could hear Hannah sniggering behind him.

'Lilly's gonna laugh her head off when she sees you in those pyjamas.'

He stopped.

'Lilly?'

'She's in the garden. She ain't hardly left your side for a minute. She slept on a truckle outside your door. Can't think why.'

He turned back so she couldn't see his face.

'Go and ask Mr Pilbury if I might have a wash out in the yard.'

'Ask him yourself.'

'Hannah!' She gave in and clumped sulkily off down the hall in the direction Pilbury had gone.

As he limped down the first flight of stairs he could hear her chattering away to Pilbury in the room that was to be hers from now on. She had entirely ignored his message and was pronouncing her opinion on the room's décor.

'Of course yellow is so much nicer than pink, and perhaps a rug here so my feet don't get cold when I climb out of bed and . . .'

He almost went back to chide her but there would be time enough for that later.

He stepped out onto the first floor.

Already the place felt different. The shutters had been flung wide and the whole house was filled with sunlight. Some of the windows were open and the musty smell of stale air and unwashed linen had been replaced by the scent of flowers. Someone had tidied up and the surfaces that had been clouded with dust were now glinting. As he went down the last flight of stairs and into the hall he could hear a woman singing to herself. Mrs Membery was in the living room, arranging a huge bunch of white roses in a vase above the fireplace. On a table by the sofa was a glass with a few dregs of milk inside, and a plate containing nothing but crumbs. Evidently she had finally found a willing recipient for all those cakes.

There would be time to say hello later.

He passed quietly down the hallway and into the kitchen. His heart sank. The woman was no longer sitting by the pond in the garden. But then a movement to his right caught his eye.

Someone was in the little glasshouse that leaned against

the eastern wall. The sun glanced off the panes too brightly for him to see inside so he let himself out of the back door and walked unsteadily down the brick path towards it.

Now he could see her. His breath caught in his throat and he stopped.

The Lilly he had known before had been a ghost of a girl. This was the flesh and blood. Her hair hung in lustrous curls down her back, tied with a crimson ribbon that matched her dress. The bodice of this new dress was tighter, and the way it clung to her shape made his skin flush with heat despite the breeze on his shoulders. Her cheeks were pinker, her lips fuller, but her eyes were the same, hidden now by her dark lashes as she looked down at something in her hands.

And then she turned those large dark eyes on him.

For a moment they simply stared at one another.

Then he walked forward, trying not to limp, trying to be strong and brave and deserving of the look on her face.

She was holding a drawing of him asleep and set it down as he approached, on a table scattered with other portraits. One was of an old woman with long white hair hanging loose on her shoulders. Titus picked it up.

'That's Florence,' Lilly said quietly. 'I wanted something to remember her by.'

Titus frowned.

'Will you not see her again?'

Lilly shook her head, smiling down at her charcoal-black fingers.

Titus went over and took them in his own. Somewhere far away Hannah was laughing and Mrs Membery was singing and the wind murmured in the trees, but all he could hear was Lilly's breathing and the soft rustle of her dress as she leaned into him. The drawing slipped from his fingers, and the last thing Titus glimpsed before he closed his eyes was its pale ghost drifting down the garden, to be lost amongst the trees.

# Acknowledgements

I'd like to thank all those who helped me along the path to publication, through their encouragement, lack of discouragement and invaluable advice.

Firstly, of course, my agent, Eve White, whose phone call that summer's afternoon so flabbergasted me I entirely forgot I had children who needed picking up from school. To brilliant editor, Shelley Instone, whose insistence that working with her would be arduous and painful proves she can be wrong on occasion after all.

Gratitude and respect to Venetia Gosling at Simon and Schuster for her consideration, patience and insight. So many others have worked on the book and I apologise for not naming them in person, but I must mention Paul Coomey, whose cover design is just gobsmackingly great.

The burden of having a budding writer's fragile ego in the family is an onerous one so thanks to all of you who have put up with me. To Daddy and Jane for their careful honesty. To my fantastic mother-in-law, Grace Squibb, for her unswerving faith in me. To Mum for her slightly unnerving degree of general knowledge and her ability to spot a good yarn.

Thanks to Bert and Bill for keeping me out of the pub and on the straight and narrow. And finally, eternal love and gratitude to Vince, who picks oakum and pounds rocks so that I can write.